Navy Brat

Navy Brat

Debbie Macomber

WHEELER
CHIVERS

This Large Print edition is published by Wheeler Publishing, Waterville, Maine USA and by BBC Audiobooks, Ltd, Bath, England.

Published in 2004 in the U.S. by arrangement with Harlequin Books S.A.

Published in 2004 in the U.K. by arrangement with Harlequin Enterprises II, B.V.

U.S. Hardcover 1-58724-680-5 (Romance)
U.K. Hardcover 0-7540-9681-5 (Chivers Large Print)
U.K. Softcover 0-7540-9682-3 (Camden Large Print)

The text of this Large Print edition is unabridged.
Other aspects of the book may vary from the original edition.

Set in 16 pt. Plantin by Myrna S. Raven.

Printed in the United States on permanent paper.

British Library Cataloguing-in-Publication Data available

Library of Congress Cataloging-in-Publication Data

Macomber, Debbie.
    Navy brat / Debbie Macomber.
        p. cm.
    ISBN 1-58724-680-5 (lg. print : hc : alk. paper)
    1. United States. Navy — Officers — Fiction.   2. Large type books.   I. Title.
PS3563.A2364N375 2004
    813′.54—dc22   2004043048

For Marcia, Catherine, Kathy and Pam
and others like them,
who've picked up the pieces of their lives
and
taught me the meaning of the word *courage*.

Special thanks to:
Gene Romano, Senior Chief Journalist,
Naval Base Seattle

Barbara Davis,
Kitsap County Community Action Program
and
The Olympic College
Women in Transition Group

Plus
navy wives
Rose Marie Harris
Jan Evans

Dear Reader,

I live in a navy town, across Sinclair inlet from the navy shipyard in Bremerton. Aircraft carriers, diesel submarines and destroyers are all part of the water view. Growing up in eastern Washington, I didn't know many navy folks. My dad was an army man who fought in WWII, and when he talked about his war experiences, it had to do with the land battles.

I know I'll never forget the first time I saw an aircraft carrier. I stood agog watching all 1092 feet of this huge flattop sail toward Bremerton. Wives, daughters, girlfriends, sons and daughters lined the wharf. The inlet was filled with sailboats and small watercraft that zigzagged across the wake, bouncing over the swelling waves the *Nimitz* created. As I stood on a hillside in Port Orchard and watched the scene below, I could feel the excitement and joy from both carrier and land. It'd been six long months since these men had been with their loved ones.

For the first time in my life I understood why my father would tear up when he saluted an American flag. In witnessing the *Nimitz* homecoming, I experienced such a surge of patriotism that I covered my heart with my hand and started to sing "God Bless America." My friend who was with me at the time asked, "What's with you?" What, my friends, were five navy books. The second of these books is titled *Navy Blues*. I wrote them all back in the late 1980s before we ever thought about e-mail or cell phones, which are in common use today.

Over the years I've been repeatedly asked when my navy books will be published again. I'm very excited to see them re-issued now. May you read them and appreciate the men and the women of our military who've dedicated themselves to our national defense. I hope you experience that surge of patriotism the way I did that bright summer's afternoon when I first laid eyes on the *Nimitz*.

God Bless America and the United States Navy.

Sincerely,

Debbie Macomber

P.S. I love hearing from my readers. You can write me at P.O. Box 1458, Port Orchard, WA 98366 or visit my Web site at www.debbiemacomber.com.

Chapter One

He was the handsomest man in the bar, and he couldn't keep his eyes off her.

It was all Erin MacNamera could do to keep her own coffee-brown eyes trained away from him. He sat on the bar stool, his back to the multitiered display of ornamental liquor bottles. His elbows were braced against the polished mahogany counter, and he nonchalantly held a bottle of imported German beer in his hand.

Against her will, Erin's gaze meandered back to him. He seemed to be waiting for her attention, and he smiled, his mouth lifting sensuously at the edges. Erin quickly looked away and tried to concentrate on what her friend was saying.

". . . Steve and me."

Erin hadn't a clue as to what she'd missed. Aimee was in the habit of talking nonstop, especially when she was upset. The reason Erin and her co-worker were meeting was that Aimee wanted to discuss the problems she was having in her ten-year marriage.

Marriage was something Erin fully intended to avoid, at least for a good long while. She was focusing her energies on her career and on teaching a class titled Women

9

in Transition two evenings a week at South Seattle Community College. With a master's degree clutched in her hot little hand, and her ideals and enthusiasm high, Erin had applied to and been accepted by the King County Community Action Program as an employment counselor, working mainly with displaced women. Ninety percent of those she worked with were on public assistance.

Her dream was to give hope and support to those who had lost both. A friend to the friendless. An encourager to the disheartened. Erin's real love, however, was the Women In Transition course. In the past few years she'd watched several women undergo the metamorphosis from lost and confused individuals to purpose-filled adults holding on tight to a second chance at life.

Erin knew better than to take the credit or the blame for the transformation she saw in these women's lives. She was just part of the Ways and Means Committee.

Her father enjoyed teasing her, claiming his eldest daughter was destined to become the next Florence Nightingale and Mother Teresa all rolled into one tenacious, determined, confident female.

Casey MacNamera was only partially right. Erin certainly didn't see herself as any crusader, fighting against the injustices of life.

Nor was Erin fooling herself about finances. She didn't intend to become wealthy,

at least not monetarily. Nobody went into social work for the money. The hours were
long and the rewards sporadic, but when she
saw people's lives turned around for good she
couldn't help being uplifted.

Helping others through a time of painful
transition was what Erin had been born to
do. It had been her dream from early in her
college career and had followed her through
graduate school and her first job.

"Erin," Aimee said, her voice dipping to a
whisper, "there's a man at the bar staring at
us."

Erin pretended not to have noticed. "Oh?"

Aimee stirred the swizzle stick in her straw-
berry daiquiri, then licked the end as she
stared across the room, her eyes studying the
good-looking man with the imported ale. Her
smile was slow and deliberate, but it didn't
last long. She sighed and said, "It's you who
interests him."

"How can you be so sure?"

"Because I'm married."

"He doesn't know that," Erin argued.

"Sure he does." Aimee uncrossed her long
legs and leaned across the minuscule table.
"Married women give off vibes, and single
men pick them up like sonar. I tried to send
him a signal, but it didn't work. He knew
immediately. You, on the other hand, are
giving off single vibes, and he's zeroing in on
that like a bee does pollen."

"I'm sure you're wrong."

"Maybe," Aimee agreed in a thin whisper, "but I doubt it." She took one last sip of her drink and stood hurriedly. "I'm leaving now, and we'll test my theory and see what happens. My guess is that the minute I'm out of here he's going to make a *beeline* for you." She paused, smiled at her own wit, then added, "The pun was an accident, clever but unintentional."

"Aimee, I thought you wanted to talk. . . ." Erin, however, wasn't quick enough to convince her friend to stay. Before she'd finished, Aimee had reached for her purse. "We'll talk some other time." With a natural flair, she draped the strap of her imitation-snakeskin handbag over her shoulder and winked suggestively. "Good luck."

"Ah . . ." Erin was at a loss as to what to do. She was twenty-seven, but for the majority of her adult life she'd avoided romantic relationships. Not by design. It had just worked out that way.

She met men frequently, but she dated only occasionally. Not once had she met a man in a bar. Cocktail lounges weren't her scene. In her entire life she'd probably been inside one only a couple of times.

Her social life had been sadly neglected from the time she was in junior high and fell in love for the first time. Howie Riverside had asked her to the Valentine's Day dance, and her tender young heart had been all aflutter.

Then it had happened. The way it always had. Her father, a career navy man, had been transferred, and they'd moved three days before the dance.

Somehow Erin had never quite regained her stride with the opposite sex. Of course, three moves in the next four years — unusual even for the navy — hadn't been exactly conducive to a thriving relationship. They'd been shuffled from Alaska to Guam to Pensacola and back again.

College could have, and probably should have, been the opportunity to make up for lost time, but by then Erin had felt like a social pygmy when it came to dealing with men. She hadn't known how to meet them, how to flirt with them or how to make small talk. Nor had she acquired a number of the other necessary graces.

"Hello."

She hadn't even had time to collect her thoughts, let alone her purse. Mr. Imported Beer was standing next to her table, smiling down on her like some mythological Greek god. He certainly resembled one. He was tall, naturally. Weren't they all? Easily six-four, she guessed, and muscular. His dark hair was neatly trimmed, his brown eyes warm and friendly. He was so handsome, he might well have posed for one of those hunk calendars that were currently the rage with all the women in the office.

"Hi," she managed, hoping she sounded a whole lot less flustered than she was feeling. Erin knew herself well, and she couldn't imagine what it was about her that had attracted this gorgeous man.

Few would have described Erin as a beautiful sophisticate. Her features were distinctively Irish, comely and appealing, but she wasn't anywhere close to being strikingly beautiful. Naturally long curly chestnut-red hair, straight white teeth and a smidgen of freckles across the bridge of her Gaelic nose were her most distinctive features. She was reasonably attractive, but no more so than any of the other women who populated the cocktail lounge.

"Do you mind if I join you?"

"Ah . . . sure." She reached for her glass of Chablis and held on to it with one hand. "And you are . . ."

"Brandon Davis." He claimed the chair recently vacated by Aimee. "Most folks call me Brand."

"Erin MacNamera," she supplied, and noticed several envious stares coming her way from the women in the crowd. Even if nothing came from this exchange, Erin couldn't help being flattered by his attention. "Most folks call me Erin."

He smiled.

"Is it true? Was I really giving off vibes?" she asked, surprising herself. Obviously it was the wine talking. Generally she wasn't even close to being this direct with a man she didn't know.

Brand didn't answer her right away, which wasn't any wonder. She'd probably caught him off guard, which was only fair, since he was throwing her completely off balance.

"My friend was saying men in bars pick up vibes like a radar detector," she explained, "and I was wondering what messages I was signaling."

"None."

"Oh." She couldn't help being disappointed. For a moment there, she'd thought she'd stumbled upon some latent talent she hadn't known she possessed. Apparently that wasn't the case.

"Then why were you staring at me?" He'd probably ruin everything by informing her she had a run in her nylons, or her skirt was unzipped, or something else thoroughly embarrassing.

"Because you're Irish and it's St. Patrick's Day."

So much for padding her ego. Naturally. It was the in thing to be seen with an Irish girl on a day that traditionally celebrated her ancestors.

"You're not wearing green," he added.

"I'm not?" Erin's gaze dropped to her blue

striped business suit. She hadn't given a thought to it being St. Patrick's Day when she'd dressed that morning. "I'm not," she agreed, surprised she'd forgotten something so basic to her heritage.

Brand laughed lightly, and the sound of it was so refreshing, Erin couldn't keep from smiling herself. She didn't know a whole lot about this sort of thing, but her best guess suggested Brand Davis wasn't the type of man who lounged around bars picking up women. First of all, he didn't need to. With his good looks and innate charm, women would naturally flock to him.

She decided to test her suspicion. "I don't believe I've seen you here before." That wasn't too surprising. Since this was her first time at the Blue Lagoon, the chances of their having crossed each other's paths at the bar were pretty slender.

"It's my first time."

"I see."

"What about you?"

It took Erin a second to realize he was asking her how often she frequented the cocktail lounge. "Every now and again," she answered, striving to sound urbane, or at least a tad more sophisticated than she'd been at age fourteen.

The waitress stepped up to the table, and before Erin could answer one way or the other Brand ordered two more of the same.

16

Generally, one glass of wine was Erin's limit, but she was willing to break a few rules. It wasn't often she ran into a Greek god.

"I'm new to the area," Brand explained before Erin could think fast enough to formulate a question.

She looked at him and smiled blandly. The wine had dulled her senses, but then, making small talk had always been difficult for her. She wished she could think of some intelligent comment to make. Instead, her gaze fell on a poster on the other side of the room, and she blurted out the first thing that came to her mind.

"I love ferries." Then, realizing he might think she was referring to leprechauns, she felt compelled to explain. "When I first moved to Seattle, I was enthralled by the ferryboats. Whenever I needed to think something over, I'd ride one over to Winslow or Bremerton and hash everything out in my mind."

"It helps?"

Whatever you do, don't let her know you're navy. Casey MacNamera's voice echoed in Brand's mind like a Chinese gong. The MCPO — masterchief petty officer — was a good friend of Brand's. They'd worked together for three years early in his career, and they'd kept in touch ever since.

As soon as Casey had learned Brand had

17

been given his special assignment at Naval Station Puget Sound at Sand Point in Seattle, the old Irishman had contacted him, concerned about his eldest daughter.

She's working too hard, not taking care of herself. Give an old man some peace of mind and check up on her. Only, for the love of heaven, don't let her know I sent you.

Personally, Brand wasn't much into this detective business. But, as a favor to his friend, he'd reluctantly agreed to look up Erin MacNamera.

He'd been ready to enter her office building when she'd stepped outside. Brand had never met Casey's daughter, but one look at that thick thatch of auburn hair and he'd immediately known that this woman was a close relative of his friend. So he'd followed her into the Blue Lagoon.

He studied her for several minutes, noticing little things about her. She was delicate. Not dainty or fragile, as the word implied. Erin MacNamera was exquisite. That wasn't a word he used often. Her gaze had met his once, and he'd managed to hold her look for just a second. She'd stared back at him, surprise darkening her eyes, before she'd jerked her gaze away. When he'd stepped up to her table, she'd been flustered, and she'd striven hard not to show it.

The more time he spent with her, the more he learned about her that amazed him. Brand wasn't entirely sure what he'd expected from Casey's daughter, but certainly not the enchanting red-haired beauty who sat across from him. Erin was as different from her old man as silk was from leather. Casey was a potbellied, boisterous MCPO, while his daughter was a graceful creature with eyes as shiny and dark as the sea at midnight.

Another thing, Casey had warned. *Remember, this is my daughter, not one of your cupcakes.*

Brand couldn't help grinning at that. He didn't have cupcakes. At thirty-two, he couldn't say he'd never been in love. He'd fallen in love a handful of times over the years, but there had never been one woman who'd captured his heart for more than a few months. None that he'd ever seriously considered spending the rest of his life with.

Be careful what you say, Casey had advised. *My Erin's got her mother's temper.*

Brand didn't feel good about this minor deception. The sensation intensified as they sat and talked over their drinks. An hour after he'd sat down with her, Erin glanced at her watch and flatly announced she had to be leaving.

As far as Brand was concerned, his duty was done. He'd looked up his friend's daughter, talked to her long enough to assure her father, when he wrote next, that Erin was in good health. But when she stood to leave, Brand discovered he didn't want her to go.

He'd thoroughly enjoyed her company.

"How about dinner?" he found himself asking.

Twin spots of color appeared in her cheeks, and her eyes darkened slightly as though she'd been caught off guard. "Ah . . . not tonight. Thanks anyway."

"Tomorrow?"

Her silence didn't fool him. She appeared outwardly calm, as if she were considering his invitation, but Brand could feel the resistance radiating from her. That in itself was unusual. Women generally were eager to date him.

"No thanks." Her soft smile took any sting out of her rejection — or at least it was meant to. Unfortunately, it didn't work.

She stood, smiled sweetly and tucked her purse under her arm. "Thanks for the drink."

Before Brand had time to respond, she was out the door. He couldn't remember a woman turning him down in fifteen years of dating. Not once. Most members of the opposite sex treated him as if he were Prince Charming. He'd certainly gone out of his way to be captivating to MacNamera's daughter.

Who the hell did she think she was?

Standing, Brand started out the cocktail lounge after her. She was halfway down the block on the sidewalk, her pace clipped. Brand ran a few steps, then slowed to a walk.

Soon his stride matched hers.

"Why?"

She paused and looked up at him, revealing no surprise that he'd joined her.

"You're navy."

Brand was shocked, and he did a poor job of disguising it. "How'd you know?"

"I was raised in the military. I know the lingo, the jargon."

"I didn't use any."

"Not consciously. It was more than that . . . the way you held your beer bottle should have told me, but it was when we started talking about the ferries crossing Puget Sound that I knew for sure."

"So I'm navy. Is that so bad?"

"No. Actually, with most women it's a plus. From what I understand, a lot of females go for guys in uniform. You won't have any problems meeting someone. Bremerton? Sand Point? Or Whidbey Island?"

Brand ignored the question of where he was stationed and instead asked one of his own. "Most women are attracted to a man in uniform, but not you?"

Her eyes flickered, and she laughed curtly. "Sorry. It lost its appeal when I was around six."

She was walking so fast that he was losing his breath just keeping up with her. "Do you hate the navy so much?"

His question apparently caught her by surprise, because she stopped abruptly, turned to him and raised wide brown eyes to study him. "I don't hate it at all."

"But you won't even have dinner with someone in the service?"

"Listen, I don't mean to be rude. You seem like a perfectly nice —"

"You're not being rude. I'm just curious, is all." He glanced around them. They'd stopped in the middle of the sidewalk on a busy street in downtown Seattle. Several people were forced to walk around them. "I really would be interested in hearing your views. How about if we find a coffee shop and sit down and talk?"

She looked at her watch pointedly.

"This isn't dinner. Just coffee." Unwilling to be put off quite so easily a second time, Brand gifted her with one of his most dazzling smiles. For the majority of his adult life, women had claimed he had a smile potent enough to melt the polar ice cap. He issued it now, full strength, and waited for the usual results.

Nothing.

This woman was downright dangerous to his ego. He tried another tactic. "In case you didn't notice, we're causing something of a traffic jam here."

"I'll pay for my own coffee," she insisted in a tone that implied she was going against her better judgment to agree to talk to him at all.

"If you insist."

The lunch counter at Woolworth's was still open, and they shared a tiny booth designed for two. While the waitress delivered their coffee, Brand reached for a menu, reading over the list of sandwiches. The picture of the turkey, piled high with lettuce and tomato slices between thick slices of bread, looked appetizing, and he reluctantly set it aside.

"Officer?" Erin asked, studying him while he stirred cream into his coffee.

"Adding cream to my coffee told you that?" Casey's daughter ought to be in intelligence. He'd never met anyone quite like her.

"No. The way you talk. The way you act. Lieutenant j.g. would be my guess?"

He was impressed again. "How'd you know that?"

"Your age. What are you, thirty? Thirty-one?"

"Thirty-two." This was getting to be downright embarrassing. He'd climbed through the ranks at the normal rate of speed and received a number of special assignments over the years. Since the navy was considering closing down its station at Sand Point, Brand had been sent by the admiral to conduct a feasibility survey. His duties in the area would last only a few weeks. Most of that time had already been spent.

"I take it you weren't raised in the navy?" Erin questioned.

"No."

"I might have guessed."

She sure as hell was batting a thousand with those guesses of hers. Her eyes briefly met his, and Brand was struck once more by how hauntingly dark they were. A spark, a hint of pain — something he couldn't quite name — touched an emotional chord deep within him.

"Listen," she said softly, regretfully, "it's been interesting talking to you, but I should have been home an hour ago." She was ready to stand when Brand reached across the table and gripped her hand.

The action was as much a shock to Brand as it was to her. She raised her head a fraction of an inch so that their eyes could meet. Hers were wide and questioning, his . . . he didn't know. Unrelenting, stubborn, he guessed. Brand wasn't thinking clearly, and hadn't been from the moment he'd followed her into the Blue Lagoon.

"We haven't talked."

"There isn't any need to. You weren't raised in the military. I was. You couldn't possibly understand what it's like unless you were carted from one corner of the world to another."

"I'd love it."

Her smile was sardonic. "Most *men* do."

"I want to see you again."

She didn't hesitate, didn't think about it. Nor did she delay answering. "No."

"I apologize if I'm bruising your ego," she added, "but frankly, I promised myself a long time ago to stay away from men in the military. It's a hard-and-fast rule I live by. Trust me, it's nothing personal."

Brand sure as hell was taking it personally. "I don't even tempt you?"

She hesitated and smiled gently before tugging her hand free from his grasp. "A little," she admitted.

Brand had the feeling she was saying that to cater to his pride, which she'd managed to bruise every time she'd opened her mouth.

"As far as looks go, you've got an interesting face."

An interesting face. Didn't she know handsome when she saw it? Women had made pests of themselves in an effort to attract his attention for years. Some of his best friends had even admitted they hesitated before introducing him to their girlfriends.

"I'll walk you to your car," he said stiffly.

"It isn't necessary, I —"

"I said I'd walk you to your car." He stood and slapped two dollar bills on the table. Brand liked to think of himself as a tolerant man, but this woman was getting under his skin, and he didn't like it. Not one damn bit. There were plenty of fish in the sea, and he was far more interested in lobster than he was in Irish stew.

Erin MacNamera wasn't even that attractive. Hell, he wouldn't even be seeing her if he wasn't doing a favor for her father. If she didn't want to see him again, fine. Great. Wonderful. He could live with that. What Erin had said earlier was true enough. Women went for guys in uniform.

He was attractive. He wore a uniform.

He didn't need Erin MacNamera.

Satisfied with that, he held open the glass door that led outside.

"This really isn't necessary," she whispered.

"Probably not, but as an officer and a gentleman I insist."

"My father's an enlisted man."

She announced the fact as if she were looking for some response.

"So?" he demanded.

"So . . . I just wanted you to know that."

"Do you think that's going to make me change my mind about walking you to your car?"

"No." Her hands were buried in her pockets. "I . . . just wanted you to know. It might make a difference to some men."

"Not me."

She nodded. "My car's in the lot near Yesler."

Brand didn't know Seattle well, but he knew enough to recognize that that area of town wasn't the best place for a woman to be walking alone at night. He was glad he'd insisted on escorting her to her car, although even now he wasn't completely sure of his motives.

They turned off the main street and onto a small, narrower one that sloped sharply down to the Seattle waterfront.

"You park here often?" As prickly as she was, Erin would probably resent his pointing out the all-too-obvious dangers of the area.

"Every day, but generally I'm gone shortly after five. It's still light then."

"Tonight?"

"Tonight," she said with a sigh, "I met you."

Brand nodded. He found the parking lot, which by now was nearly deserted. The spaces were tightly angled between two brick buildings. The entire lot was illuminated by a single dim light.

Erin pulled her keys from her purse and clenched them in her hands. "My car is the one in the back," she explained.

Brand's gaze located the small blue Toyota in the rear of the lot, facing a two-story brick structure. Once more he was forced to swallow a chastising warning.

"I didn't want to say anything earlier, but I'm grateful you walked with me."

A small — damn small — sense of satisfaction filled him. "You're welcome."

She inserted the key into the driver's door and unlocked her car. Pausing, she glanced up at him and smiled shyly.

Brand looked down on the slender young woman at his side and read her confusion and her regret. The desire to pull her close was so strong that it was nearly impossible to ignore.

"I'm sorry the navy hurt you."

"It didn't. Not as much as I led you to believe. I just want to be on the safe side. For the first time in my life I have a real home with real furniture that I purchased without thinking about how well it would travel." She hesitated and smiled. "I don't worry about being transferred every other year, and —" She hesitated again and shook her head as though to suggest he wouldn't understand. "I apologize if I wounded your ego. You're really very nice."

"A kiss would go a long way toward repairing the damage." Brand couldn't believe he'd suggested that, but what the hell. Why not?

"A kiss?"

Brand nearly laughed out loud at the shocked look that came over her features. It was downright comical, as if she'd never been kissed before, or at least it had been a good long while. Not taking the time to decide which it was, he cradled her face between his large hands.

Her mouth was moist and parted, welcoming. Her eyes weren't. They were filled with doubts, but he chose to ignore her unspoken questions, fearing that if he took the time to reassure her he'd talk himself out of kissing her.

Brand wanted this kiss.

If Erin had questions, he was experiencing a few of his own. She was his friend's daughter, and he was risking Casey's wrath with this little game. But none of that seemed to matter. What did concern him was the woman staring boldly up at him.

Tenderness filled him. A strange tenderness, one he didn't fully understand or recognize. Slowly he lowered his mouth to hers. He felt her go tense with anticipation as their lips clung.

She was soft, warm and incredibly sweet. He opened his mouth a little more, slanting his lips over hers as he plowed his fingers through her thick hair.

Her first response was tentative, as if she'd been caught unprepared, but then she sighed and sagged against him. She flattened her hands over his chest, then flexed her fingers, her long nails scraping his sweater.

Gradually she opened to him, like a hothouse flower blossoming in his arms. Yet it was she who broke the contact. Her eyes were wide and soft as she stared up at him. A feeling of surprise and tenderness and need washed through him.

"I . . . was just thinking," she said in a lacy whisper.

Just now, thinking could be dangerous. Brand knew that from experience. He silenced her with a kiss that was so thorough it left them both trembling in its aftermath.

Once again, Erin was clinging to him, her hands gripping the V of his sweater as if she needed to hold on to something in order to remain upright.

"The rules you have about dating military men?" he asked, rubbing his open mouth over her honeyed lips. "How about altering them?"

"Altering them?" she echoed slowly, her eyes closed.

He kissed her again for good measure. "Make it a guideline instead," he suggested.

Chapter Two

As an adult, Erin had made several decisions about how she intended to live her life. She followed the Golden Rule, and she never used her credit cards if she couldn't pay off the balance the following month.

And she didn't date men in the military.

Her life wasn't encumbered with a lot of restrictions. Everything that was important and necessary was wrapped up in these relatively simple rules.

Then why, she asked herself, had she agreed to have dinner with Brand Davis? Lieutenant Davis, J.G., she reminded herself disparagingly.

"Why?" she repeated aloud, stacking papers against the edge of her desk with enough force to bend them in half.

"Heavens, don't ask me," Aimee answered, grinning impishly. After a day spent interviewing job applicants, talking aloud to oneself was an accepted form of behavior.

"I'm supposed to meet him tonight, you know," Erin said in a low, thought-filled voice. If there had been an easy way out of this, she'd have grabbed it.

If only Brand hadn't kissed her. No one had ever told her kissing could be so . . . so

31

pleasant. First her knees had gone weak, and then her formidable will of iron had melted and pooled at her feet. Before she'd even realized what she was doing, she'd mindlessly walked into Brand's trap. It was just like a navy man to zero in on her weakest point and attack.

Rolling her antique oak chair away from her desk, Aimee relaxed against its rail back and angled her head to one side as she studied Erin. "Are you still lamenting the fact you agreed to have dinner with that gorgeous hunk? Honey, trust me in this, you should be counting your blessings."

"He's military."

"I know." Aimee rotated a pen between her hands as she gazed dreamily into the distance. A contented look stole over her features as she released a long-drawn-out sigh. "I can just picture him in a uniform, standing at attention. Why, it's enough to make my heart go pitter-patter."

Erin refused to look at her friend. If Aimee wanted Brand, she was welcome to him. Of course, her friend wasn't truly interested, since she was already married to Steve and had been for a decade. "If I could think of a plausible excuse to get out of this, I would."

"You've got to be kidding."

She wasn't. "You have dinner with him."

Aimee shook her head eagerly. "Trust me,

if I were five years younger I'd take you up on that."

Since Aimee's marriage was going through some rocky times, Erin didn't think it was necessary to remind her friend that dating wasn't something that should interest her.

"Relax, would you?" Aimee admonished her.

"I can't." Erin tucked her stapler and several pens neatly inside her desk drawer. "As far as I'm concerned, this evening is going to be a total waste of time." She could be doing something important, like . . . like laundry or answering mail. It was just her luck that Brand had suggested Wednesday night. Tuesday was the first class for the new session for the Women In Transition course. Thursday night was the second session. Naturally, Brand had chosen to ask her out the one night of the week when she was free.

"You're so tense," Aimee chastised. "You might as well be walking around in a suit of armor."

"I'll be okay," Erin said, not listening to her fellow worker. She stood and planted her hands against the side of her desk before sighing heavily. "This is what I'm going to do. I'll meet him just the way we arranged."

"That's a good start," Aimee teased.

"We'll find a restaurant, and I'll order right away, eat and then make my excuses as soon as I can. I don't want to insult him, but at the same time I want him to understand I regret ever having agreed to this date." She waited for a response. When Aimee didn't give her one, she arched her brows expectantly. "Well?"

"It sounds good to me." But the look Aimee gave her said otherwise.

It was amazing how much a person could say with a look. Erin didn't want to take the time to dwell on the fact, especially now, when she was thinking about the messages she'd given Brand the night he'd kissed her. Apparently she'd encouraged him enough to ask her out to dinner a second time.

Erin didn't want to dwell on that night. It embarrassed her to think about the way she'd responded so openly to his touch. Her face grew hot just remembering. She shouldn't think about it — she was running late as it was. Reaching for her purse, she checked her watch and hurried toward the elevator.

"Don't get started in the morning until we've had a chance to talk," Aimee called out after her.

They generally clocked in at eight, reviewed files and then spent a large portion of the day with job applicants or meeting with prospective employers. Sometimes she wasn't back in the office until after four.

"I won't," Erin promised without looking back. Walking briskly, she raised her hand in farewell.

"Have a good time," Aimee called out in a provocative, teasing tone that attracted the notice of their peers.

This time Erin did turn back to discover her co-worker sitting on the edge of her desk, her arms folded, one leg swinging. A mischievous grin brightened her round, cheerful face.

But Erin wasn't counting on this evening being much fun.

Once outside the revolving glass door of the tall office complex, Erin paused and glanced around. Brand had said he'd be waiting for her there. She didn't see him right away, and she was beginning to think he wasn't going to show.

It must have been wishful thinking on her part, because no sooner had the thought entered her mind than he stepped away from the building and sauntered toward her.

His gaze found hers, and Erin was struck afresh by what a devilishly handsome man Brandon Davis was. If she wasn't careful, she might find herself attracted to him. She wasn't immune to good looks and charm, and they seemed to ooze from every pore of his muscular body.

"Hi," she greeted stiffly. Her defenses were in place as she deliberately kept her eyes trained away from his smile. It was compelling enough to dazzle the most stouthearted. Erin hadn't had enough experience with the opposite sex to build up a resistance to a man like Brand.

"I wasn't sure you'd show," he said when he reached her side.

"I wasn't sure I would, either." That was stretching the truth. She was a navy brat. Responsibility, promptness and duty had been programmed into her the way most children were taught to brush their teeth and make their beds. No one could live on a military base and not be affected by the value system promoted there.

"I'm glad you did decide to meet me." His eyes were warm and genuine, and she hurriedly looked away before she could be affected by them.

"Where would you like to eat?" To Erin's way of thinking, the sooner they arrived at the restaurant, the sooner she could leave. She wanted this evening to be cut-and-dried, without a lot of room for discussion.

"Ever been to Joe's Grill?"

Erin's gaze widened with delight. "Yes, as a matter of fact, I have, but it's been years." Since she was ten by her best guess. Her father had been stationed at Sand Point, and whenever there was something to celebrate he'd taken the family out to eat at Joe's. Generally restaurants weren't something a child would remember, but it seemed her family had a special place in each of the cities where they'd been stationed through the years. Joe's Grill had been their Seattle favorite.

"I asked around and heard the food there is great," Brand said, placing his hand at her elbow.

She felt his touch, and although it was light and impersonal it still affected her. "You mean the guys from Sand Point still eat there?"

"Apparently so."

A flood of happy memories filled Erin's mind. For her tenth birthday, Joe himself had baked her a double-decker chocolate cake. She could still remember him proudly carrying it out of the kitchen as if he'd been asked to give away the bride. Visiting the restaurant had crossed her mind half a dozen times since she'd moved to Seattle, but with her hectic schedule she hadn't gotten around to it.

"Joe's Grill," she repeated, fighting the strong desire to fill in the details about her birthday and the cake to Brand. Her eyes met his, and mutual smiles emerged, despite Erin's attempts to the contrary. She had to keep her head out of the clouds when it came to dealing with this handsome lieutenant j.g. Reminding herself of that was apparently something that was going to be necessary all evening.

Brand's car was parked on a side street. He held open the passenger door for her and gently closed it once she was inside.

He did most of the talking as he drove to the restaurant. Every once in a while Erin would feel herself start to relax in his company, a sure sign she was headed for trouble. She'd give herself a hard mental shake and instantly put herself back on track.

When Brand eased the vehicle into Joe's crowded parking lot, Erin looked around her and nearly drowned in nostalgia. She swore the restaurant hadn't changed in nearly twenty years. The same neon sign flashed from above the flat-topped roof, with a huge T-bone steak lit up in red and *Joe's Grill* flashing off and on every two seconds.

"As I recall, the steaks here are so thick they resemble roasts, and the baked potatoes were larger than a boxer's fist." She was confident that was an exaggeration, but in her ten-year-old mind that was the way it seemed.

"That's what my friend said," Brand said, climbing out of the car.

The inside was much as Erin remembered. A huge fish tank built into the wall was filled with a wide variety of colorful saltwater fish. The cash register rested on top of a large glass display case full of tempting candy and gum. Erin never had understood why a restaurant that served wonderful meals would want to sell candy to its customers afterward.

The hostess escorted them to a table by a

picture window that revealed a breath-taking panorama of Lake Union.

Erin didn't open her menu right away. Instead, she looked around, soaking up the ambience, feeling as if she were a kid all over again.

"This reminds me of a little place on Guam," Brand said, his gaze following hers. "The tables have the same red tablecloths under a glass covering."

"Not . . ." She had to stop and think.

"The Trattoria," Brand supplied.

"Yes." Erin was impressed he'd even heard of it, but then he probably had since everyone stationed on Guam ate there at one time or another. "They serve a clam spaghetti my father swore he would die for. My mom tried for years to duplicate the recipe and finally gave up. Who would ever believe a tiny restaurant on the island of Guam would serve the best Italian food in the world?"

"Better even than Miceli's in Rome?" he probed.

"You've been to Miceli's?" she asked excitedly. Obviously he had, otherwise he wouldn't have mentioned it. The fresh-from-the-oven-bread was what she remembered about Miceli's. The aroma would drift through the narrow cobblestoned streets of the Italian town like nothing Erin had ever known. Her stomach growled just thinking about it.

"I've been in the navy nearly fifteen years," he reminded her.

Mentioning the fact that he was navy was like slapping a cold rag across her face and forcing her back to reality. Her reaction was immediate. She reached for the menu, jerked it open and decided what she intended to order in three seconds flat. She looked up, hoping to catch the waitress's eye.

"I can't decide if I'm hungry enough for the T-bone or not," Brand remarked conversationally. He glanced over the menu a second time before looking to her. "You've decided?"

"Yes. I'll have the peppercorn filet."

Brand nodded, apparently saluting her choice. "That sounds good. I'll have the same."

"No," Erin said, surprised by how adamant she sounded. "Have the T-bone. It's probably the best of any place in town. And since you're only going to be in Seattle a few weeks, you really should sample Joe's specialty."

"All right, I will." Brand smiled at her, and Erin's heart started to pound like a giant sledgehammer, a fact she chose to ignore.

The waitress arrived to take their order, and Brand suggested a bottle of wine.

"No, thanks, none for me," Erin said quickly. After what had happened the night they'd met, she'd considered living her entire life without drinking wine again. It was probably ridiculous to blame two glasses of Chablis for the eager way she'd responded to Brand's kisses. But it was an excuse, and she badly needed one. She certainly wasn't looking for a repeat performance. Her objective was to get through this dinner, thank Brand and then go her own way. Naturally she wanted them to part with the understanding she didn't ever intend to date him again. But she wanted to be sure he realized it was nothing personal.

The conversation that followed was polite, if a tad stilted. Erin's hand circled the water glass, and her gaze flittered across the restaurant, gathering in the memories.

"I made a mistake," Brand announced out of the blue, capturing her attention. "I shouldn't have reminded you I'm navy. You were enjoying yourself until then."

Erin lowered her gaze to the red linen napkin in her lap. "Actually, I'm grateful. It's far too easy to forget with you." As she spoke, Erin could hear a thread of resentment and fear in her own voice.

"I was hoping we might be able to forget about that."

"No," she answered, softly, regretfully. "I can't allow myself to forget. You're here for how long? Two, three weeks?" She asked this as a reminder to herself of how foolish it would be to become involved with Brand.

"Two weeks."

"That's what I thought." Her gaze drifted toward the kitchen in a silent appeal to the chef to hurry with their order. The more time she spent with Brand, the more susceptible she was to his charm. He was everything she feared. Appealing. Attractive. *Charming.* She was beginning to hate that word, but it seemed to fit him so well.

He asked her about the places she'd lived, and she answered him as straightforwardly as she could, trying not to let the resentment seep into her voice. Her answers were abridged, clipped.

Their meal arrived, and none too soon, as far as Erin was concerned.

Brand's steak was delicious. As delicious as Erin had promised, cooked to perfection. He didn't know what to make of Erin MacNamera, however. Hell, he didn't know what to make of himself. She'd made her views on seeing him plain enough. He didn't know what it was about her that affected him so strongly. The challenge, perhaps. There weren't many women who turned him down flat the way she had.

The challenge was there, he'd admit that, but it was something else, too. Something he couldn't quite put his finger on. Whatever it was, Erin was driving him crazy.

They'd agreed to meet outside her office

building, and Brand had half expected her to stand him up. When she had shown, he'd noted regretfully that it wasn't out of any desire to spend time with him. At first she'd been tense. They'd started talking, and she'd lowered her guard and been beginning to relax. Then he'd blown it by reminding her he was in the navy.

From that point on he might as well have been sitting across the table from a robot. He'd asked her something, and she'd answered him with one-word replies or by simply shrugging her shoulders. After a while he'd given up the effort. If she wanted conversation with her dinner, then she could damn well carry it on her own.

It didn't come as any surprise to Brand that she was ready to leave the minute they finished. He collected the bill, left a generous tip and escorted Erin to the car.

"Are you parked at the same lot off Yesler?" he asked once they were in traffic.

"Yes. You can drop me off there, if you don't mind."

"I don't." Brand noted that she sounded downright eager to part company with him. This woman was definitely a detriment to his ego. Fine, he got the message. He wasn't exactly sure why he'd even suggested this dinner date. As Erin had taken pains to remind him, he would be in Seattle only a couple of weeks. The implication being that he'd be out of her life forever then. Apparently that was exactly what she wanted.

In retrospect, Brand was willing to admit why he'd asked her out to dinner.

It was the kiss.

Her response, so tentative in the beginning, so hesitant and unsure, had thrown him for a loop. If Casey was ever to find out Brand had kissed his red-haired daughter, there would be hell to pay. The sure wrath of his friend hadn't altered the fact Brand had wanted to kiss Erin. And kiss her he had, until his knees had been knocking and his heart had been roaring like a runaway train.

What had started out as a challenge had left him depleted and shaken. Numb with surprise and wonder. Erin had flowered in his arms like a rare tropical plant. She was incredibly sweet, and so soft that he'd been forced to use every ounce of restraint he possessed not to crush her in his arms.

This dinner date was a different story. She could hardly wait to get out of his car. Fine. He'd let her go, because frankly he wasn't much into cultivating a relationship with a woman who clearly didn't want to have anything to do with him.

He pulled off First Avenue onto the lot and left the engine running, hoping she'd get his message, as well.

Her hand was already closed around the door handle. "Thank you for dinner."

44

"You're welcome," was his stiff reply. His tone bordered on the sarcastic, but if she noticed she didn't comment.

"I'm sorry I was such poor company."

He didn't claim otherwise. She hesitated, and for a wild moment Brand thought she might lean over and gently kiss him goodbye. It would have been a nice gesture on her part.

She didn't.

Instead she scooted out of the car, fiddled with the snap of her purse and retrieved her key chain, all while he sat waiting for her. When she'd opened the door to her Toyota, she twisted around and smiled sadly, as if she wanted to say something more. She didn't, however. She just climbed inside resolutely.

Brand had to back up his car in order for her to pull out of the parking space. He did so with ease, reversing his way directly into the street. She came out after him and headed in the opposite direction.

His hand tightened around the steering wheel as she drove off into the night.

"Goodbye, Erin. We might have been friends," he murmured, and regret settled over his shoulders like a heavy wool jacket.

Once he was back at his room in the officers' quarters, Brand showered and climbed into bed. He read for a while, but the novel, which had been touted as excellent, didn't hold his interest. After fifteen minutes, he turned out the light.

He should have kissed her.

The thought flashed through his mind like a shot from a ray gun.

Hell, no. It was apparent Erin didn't want to have anything to do with him. Wonderful. Great. He was man enough to accept her decision.

Forcefully, he punched up the pillow under his head and closed his eyes.

Before he realized what he was doing, a slight smile curved his lips. She should count herself lucky he hadn't taken it upon himself to prove her wrong and kiss her again. If he had, she would have been putty in his hands, just the way she had been the first time. Erin MacNamera might well have believed she had the situation under control, but she hadn't. She'd been tense and uneasy, and for no other reason than the fear that Brand was going to take her in his arms again.

He should have. He'd wanted to. Until now he hadn't been willing to admit how damn much he had longed to taste her again.

Brand rolled over onto his stomach and nuzzled his face into the thick softness of the pillow. Erin had been feather-soft. When she'd moved against him, her breasts had lightly cushioned his chest. The memory of her softness clouded his mind.

Burying his face in the pillow added fuel to his imagination, and he abruptly rolled over.

He firmly shut his eyes and sighed as he started to drift off.

It didn't work. Instead, he saw Erin's sweet Irish face looking back at him.

Her eyes were an unusual shade of brown. Man-enticing brown, he decided. With her curly red hair and her pale, peach-smooth complexion, her eye color was something of a surprise. He'd expected blue or green, not dark brown.

Beautiful brown eyes . . . so readable, so clear, looking back at him, as if she were suffering from a wealth of regrets just before she'd climbed into her car.

Brand was suffering from a few regrets of his own. He hadn't kissed her. Nor had he suggested they see each other again.

Damn his pride. He should have done something, anything, to persuade her. Now she was gone. . . .

Sleep danced around him until he was on the verge of drifting off completely. Then his eyes snapped open, and a slow, satisfied smile turned up the edges of his mouth.

He knew exactly what he intended to do.

Erin remembered Marilyn Amundson from the first session of the Women in Transition course on Tuesday evening. The middle-aged woman with pain-dulled blue eyes and fashionably styled hair had sat at the back of the room, in the last row. Throughout most of the class, she'd kept her gaze lowered. Erin noted that the woman took copious notes as she outlined the sixteen-session course. Every now and again, the older woman would pause, dab a tissue at the corner of her eyes and visibly struggle to maintain her aplomb.

At nine, when class was dismissed, Marilyn had slowly gathered her things and hurried outside the classroom. Later Erin had seen a car stop in front of the college to pick her up.

It was Erin's guess that Marilyn didn't drive. It wasn't unusual for the women who signed up for the course to have to rely on someone else for transportation.

Most of the women were making a new life for themselves. Some came devastated by divorce, others from the death of a loved one. Whatever the reason, they all shared common ground and had come to learn and help each other. When the sessions were finished, the classes continued to meet as a monthly support group.

The greatest rewards Erin had had as a social worker were from the Women in Transition course. The transformation she'd seen in the participants' lives in the short two months she taught the class reminded her of the metamorphosis of a cocoon into a butterfly.

The first few classes were always the most difficult. The women came feeling empty in-

48

side, fearful, tormented by the thought of facing an unknown future. Many were angry, some came guilt-ridden, and there were always a few who were restless, despairing and pessimistic.

What a good portion of those who signed up for the course didn't understand when they first arrived was how balanced life was. Whenever there was a loss, the stage was set for something to be gained. A new day was born, the night was lost. A flower blossomed, the bud was lost. In nature and in all aspects of life an advantage could be found in a loss. A balance, oftentimes not one easily explained or understood, but a symmetry nevertheless, was waiting to be discovered and explored. It was Erin's privilege to teach these women to look for the gain.

"I was wondering if I could talk to you?"

Erin paused. "Of course. You're Marilyn Amundson?"

"Yes." The older woman reached for a tissue and ran it beneath her nose. Her fingers were trembling, and it was several moments before she spoke. "I can't seem to stop crying. I sit in class and all I do is cry. . . . I want to apologize for that."

"You don't need to. I understand."

Marilyn smiled weakly. "Some of the other women in class look so . . . like they've got it all together, while I'm a basket case. My husband . . ." She paused when her voice faltered. "He asked me for a divorce two weeks ago. We've been married over thirty years. Apparently he met someone else five or six years ago, and they've been seeing each other ever since . . . only I didn't know."

This was a story Erin had heard several times over, but it wouldn't lessen Marilyn's pain for Erin to imply that she was another statistic. What she did need to hear was that others had survived this ordeal, and so would she.

"I'd . . . gone out shopping. The bus stops right outside our house, and when I returned home, Richard was there. I knew right away something was wrong. Richard only rarely wears his suit. I asked him what he was doing home in the middle of the day, and all he could do was stand there and stare at me. Then . . . then he said he was sorry to do it this way, and he handed me the divorce papers. Just like that — without any warning. I didn't know about the other woman. . . . I suppose I should have, but I . . . I trusted him."

Erin's heart twisted at the torment that echoed in the other woman's voice. Marilyn struggled to hold back the tears, her lips quivering with the effort.

"Although this may feel like the worst moment of your life, you will survive," Erin said gently, hugging her briefly. "I promise you that. The healing process is like everything else, there's a beginning, a middle and an end. It feels like the whole world has caved in on you now."

"That's exactly the way I feel. Richard is my whole life . . . was my whole life. I just don't know what I'm going to do."

"Have you seen an attorney?"

Marilyn shook her head. "Not yet . . . My pastor suggested I take this course, and find my footing, so to speak."

"In session twelve a lawyer will visit the class. You can ask any questions you like then."

"I wanted to thank you, too," Marilyn went on, once she'd composed herself. "What you said about the balance of things, how nature and life even things out . . . well, it made a lot of sense to me. Few things do these days."

Erin reached for her coat, slipping her arms into the satin-lined sleeves. She smiled, hoping the gesture would offer Marilyn some reassurance. "I'm pleased you're finding the class helpful."

"I don't think I could have made it through this last week without it." She retreated a few steps and smiled again. This time it came across stronger. "Thank you again."

"You're welcome. I'll see you Tuesday."

"I'll be here." Buttoning up her own coat, Marilyn headed out the classroom door.

Erin watched the older woman. Her heart ached for Marilyn, but, although she was devastated and shaky now, Erin saw in her a deep inner strength. Marilyn hadn't realized it was there, not yet. Soon she would discover it and draw upon the deep pool of courage. For now her thoughts were full of self-condemnation, self-deprecation and worry. From experience, Erin knew Marilyn would wallow in those for a while, but the time would come when she'd pick herself up by the bootstraps. Then that inner strength, the grit she saw in the other woman's weary eyes, would come alive.

As if sensing Erin's thoughts, Marilyn paused at the classroom door and turned back. "Do you mind if I ask you a personal question?"

"Sure, go ahead."

"Have you ever been in love?"

"No," Erin answered, regretfully. "Not even close, I'm afraid."

Marilyn nodded, then squared her shoulders. "Don't ever let it happen," she advised gruffly, yet softly. "It hurts too damn much."

Chapter Three

The envelope arrived at Erin's office, hand-delivered by the downstairs receptionist. Erin stared at her name scrawled across the front and knew beyond a doubt the handwriting belonged to Brand Davis. She held the plain white envelope in her hand several moments, her heart pounding. It'd been two days since her dinner date with Brand, and she hadn't been able to stop thinking about him. She'd been so awful, so aloof and unfriendly, when he'd been trying so hard to be cordial and helpful.

When he'd dropped her off where she'd parked her car, she'd practically leaped out of his in her eagerness to get away from him. Exactly what had he done that was so terrible? Well, first off, he'd been pleasant and fun — horrible crimes, indeed — while she'd behaved like a cantankerous old biddy. She wasn't proud of herself; in fact, Erin felt wretched about the whole thing.

"Go ahead and open it," she said aloud.

"You talking to yourself again?" Aimee chastised. "You generally don't do that until the end of the day."

"Brand sent me a note." She held it up for her friend's inspection as though she were

53

holding on to a hand grenade and expected it to explode in her face at any moment.

"I thought the receptionist looked envious. He's probably downstairs waiting for you right now."

"Ah . . ." That thought didn't bear contemplating.

"For heaven's sake," Aimee said eagerly, "don't just sit there, open it."

Erin did, with an enthusiasm she didn't dare question. Her gaze scanned the short message before she looked up to her friend. "He wants to give me a tour of Sand Point before the opportunity is gone. You know there's a distinct possibility the navy may close down the base. He says I should have a look at it for nostalgia's sake."

"When?"

"Tomorrow . . . You're right, he's downstairs waiting for my answer."

"Are you going to do it?" Aimee's question hung in mid-air like a dangling spider.

Erin didn't know. Then she did know. Longing welled deep within her, not a physical longing, but an emotional stirring that left her feeling empty inside. She didn't want to have anything to do with this lieutenant j.g., didn't want to be trapped in the whirlpool of his strong, sensual appeal. Nevertheless, she had been from the first moment they'd kissed, despite her best efforts.

He paralyzed her; he challenged her. He

was everything she claimed she didn't want in a man, and everything she'd ever hope to find.

"Well?" Aimee probed. "What are you going to do?"

"I . . . I'm going to take that tour."

Aimee let loose with a loud cheer that attracted the attention of nearly everyone in the huge open room. Several people stuck their heads out from behind office doors to discover what was causing all the excitement.

Shaking on the inside, but outwardly composed, Erin took the elevator to the ground floor. Brand was waiting in the foyer. He had his back to her and was standing in front of the directory. He wore his dress uniform, and his hands were joined behind his back, holding his garrison cap.

He must have sensed her presence, because he turned around.

"Hello," she said, her heart as heavy as the humid air of the rainy Seattle morning.

"Hi," he responded, his own voice low and throaty.

She dropped her gaze, unexpectedly nervous. "I got your note."

"You look surprised to hear from me."

"After the way I behaved the other night, I didn't expect to . . . I can't understand why you want anything to do with me."

"You weren't so bad." His lazy grin took a long time coming, but when it did it contradicted every word he'd spoken.

She found his smile infectious and doubted any woman could resist this man when he put his mind to it — and his mind was definitely to it!

"Are you free tomorrow?"

"And if I said I wasn't?" She answered him with a question of her own, thinking that was safer than admitting how pleased she was to see him.

"I'd ask you out again later."

"Why?" Erin couldn't understand why he'd continue to risk rejection from her. Especially when she was quite ordinary. Erin wasn't selling herself short. She was a warm, generous person, but she hadn't been with him. Yet he'd returned twice now, enduring her disdain, and she had yet to understand why.

Gradually she raised her eyes to his. And what she viewed confused her even more. Brand was thinking and feeling the same things she was, the same bewilderment, the same confusion. The same everything.

The smile faded, and his face tightened slightly, as if this were a question he'd often asked himself. "Why do I keep coming back?" He leveled his gaze on her. "I wish the hell I knew. Will you come to Sand Point tomorrow?"

Erin nodded, then emphasized her response by saying, "Yes. At ten?"

"Perfect." Then he added with a slight

smile, "There'll be a pass waiting for you at the gate."

"Good," she said, taking a step back, feeling nervous and not knowing how to explain it. "I'll see you tomorrow, then."

"Tomorrow."

It wasn't until Erin was inside the elevator, a smile trembling on her lips, that she remembered Marilyn's parting words from the night before.

Don't ever fall in love, Marilyn had warned her, *it hurts too damn much.* Erin felt somewhat comforted to realize she was a long way from falling in love with Brand Davis. But she would definitely have to be careful.

"Well, is it the way you remembered?" Brand asked after a two-hour tour of Naval Station Puget Sound at Sand Point. He'd given her a history lesson, too. Sand Point had originally been acquired by King County back in 1920 as an airport and later leased to the navy as a reserve. Brand had explained that only a few hundred men were based there now, support personnel for the base at Everett. Brand was assigned to the admiral's staff — SINCPAC, out of Hawaii — and sent to do an independent study in preparation for the possible closure of the base.

Erin had been on the base itself only a handful of times as a child. It amazed her how familiar the base felt to her, even though it had been sixteen years since she'd moved away from the area.

"It hasn't changed all that much over the years."

"That surprises you?"

"Not really." What did catch her unawares was the feeling of homecoming. There had never been one single base her family had been assigned to through the years that gave Erin this sort of abstract feeling of home. From the time she could remember, her life had belonged to the navy. Her father would receive shipping orders, and without a pause her family would pack up everything they owned and head wherever her father's commanding officer decreed. Erin had hated it with a fierceness that went beyond description. Nothing was ever her own, there was no sense of permanency in her life, no sense of security. What she had one day — her friends, her school, her neighbors — could be taken from her the next.

Brand's fingers reached for hers and squeezed tightly. "You look sad."

"I do?" She forced a note of cheerfulness into her voice, needing to define her feelings. Brand had brought her here. For the first time since she'd left her family, she'd returned to a navy base. She'd agreed to Brand's suggestion of a tour with flippant disregard for any emotions she might experience.

The wounds of her youth, although she knew she was being somewhat melodramatic to refer to them that way, had been properly bandaged with time. She'd set the course of her life and hadn't looked back since. Then, out of the blue, Brand Davis had popped in, determined, it seemed, to untie the compress so carefully wrapped around her heart.

As she stood outside the Sand Point grounds, she could almost feel the bandages slackening. Her first instinct was to tug them back into place, but she couldn't do that with the memories. Happy memories, carefree memories, came at her from every angle. The longer she stood there, the longer she soaked in the feelings, the more likely the bandage was to drop to her feet. Erin couldn't allow that to happen.

"I'd forgotten how much I enjoyed living in Seattle," she whispered, barely aware she was speaking.

"Where were you stationed afterward?"

Erin had to think about it. "Guam, as I recall. . . . No, we went to Alaska first."

"You hated it there?"

"Not exactly. Don't get me wrong, it wasn't my favorite place in the world, but it was tolerable. . . . We weren't there long." The sun actually did shine at midnight, and the mosquito was teasingly referred to as the Alaska state bird. Actually, Erin had loved Alaska, but they'd been there such a short while.

"How long?"

"Four months, I'd guess. There was some screwup, and almost overnight we were given orders and shipped to Guam. Now that was one place I really did enjoy."

"Did you ever take picnics on Guam?"

Erin had to think that one over, and she couldn't actually remember one way or the other. "I suppose we did."

"And how did you enjoy those?"

Erin glanced in Brand's direction and studied him through narrowed eyes. "Why do I have the funny feeling this is a leading question?"

"Because it is." Brand grinned at her, and the sun broke through whatever clouds there were that day. "I packed us a lunch, and I was hoping to persuade you to go on a picnic with me."

"Where?" Not that it mattered. The question was a delaying tactic to give her time to sort through her scattered feelings. A tour of Sand Point was one thing, but lying down on the grass feeding each other grapes was another.

"Anywhere you want."

"Ah?" Her mind scurried as she tried to come up with the names of parks, but for the life of her Erin couldn't remove the picture of Brand pressing a grape to her lips and then bending over to kiss her and share the juicy flavor.

"Erin?"

"How about Woodland Park? If you haven't visited the zoo, you should. Seattle has one of the country's best." That way she could feed the animals and take her mind off Brand. The choice was a good one for another reason, as well. Woodland Park was sure to be crowded on a day as bright and sunny as this one.

Erin was right. They were fortunate to find parking. Brand frowned as he glanced around them, and she could almost hear his thoughts. He'd been hoping she'd lead him to a secluded hideaway, and she'd greatly disappointed him. He might as well become accustomed to it. Erin had agreed to see him again, but she absolutely refused to become romantically involved.

"Just who do you think you're kidding?" she muttered under her breath. Her stomach had been tied up in knots for the last hour while she'd replayed over and over again in her mind this ridiculous scene about them sharing grapes. For all she knew, he might have brought along apples, or oranges, or omitted fruit altogether.

"You said something?" Brand asked, giving her an odd look.

"No . . ."

"I thought you did."

She was going to have to examine this need to talk out loud to herself. As far as she could see, the best tactic was to change the subject. "I'm starved."

"Me too." But when he glanced her way, his gaze rested squarely on her mouth, as if to say he was eager to eat all right, but his need wasn't for food.

Her beautiful Irish eyes were moody, Brand decided. Moody and guarded. Brand didn't know what he'd done — or hadn't done — that disturbed Erin so much. From the moment they'd driven away from the naval station, he'd toyed with the idea of asking her what was wrong. He hadn't, simply because he knew she'd deny that anything was troubling her.

Brand wasn't pleased with her choice of parks for their picnic. The zoo was a place for family and kids. He'd be lucky if they found five minutes alone together. But then, that was exactly the reason Erin had chosen it.

Brand, on the other hand, wanted seclusion and privacy. He wanted to kiss Erin again. Hell, he *needed* to kiss Erin again. The thought had dominated his mind for days. She was so incredibly soft and sweet. He swore he'd never kissed another woman who tasted of honey the way she did. The sample she'd given him hadn't been nearly enough to satisfy his need. For days he'd been telling himself he'd blown the kiss up in his mind, way out of proportion. Nothing could have been that good.

"Anyplace around here will do," she said.

He followed her into the park, his gaze scanning the rolling green landscape and falling on a large pond. The space under the trees near the shore looked the most promising. He suggested there.

"Sure," she responded, but she sounded uncertain.

Brand smoothed out the gray navy-issue blanket on the lawn and set the wicker basket in the center of it.

"If you'd said something earlier, I would have baked brownies," Erin said, striving, Brand thought, to sound conversational.

"You can next time." The implication was there, as blatant as he could make it. He would be seeing her again. Often. As frequently as their schedules allowed. He planned on it, and he wanted her to do the same.

"What did you pack for us?" Her voice sounded hollow, as if it were coming from an abandoned well.

"Nothing all that fabulous." Kneeling on the blanket, he opened the basket and set out sandwiches, a couple of cans of cold pop, potato chips and two oranges.

Erin's gaze rested on the oranges for the longest moment. They were the large Florida variety, juicy, she suspected, and sweet.

"Do you want the turkey on white or the

63

corned beef on whole wheat?"

"The turkey," she answered.

Next Brand opened the chips and handed her the bag. She grabbed a handful and set them on top of a napkin. For all her claims about being famished, Brand noted, she barely touched her food.

He sat, leaning his back against the base of the tree, and stretched his long legs out in front of him, crossing his ankles. "You're looking thoughtful."

Her responding smile was weak. "I . . . I was just thinking about something one of the women in my class told me."

"What was that?"

Her head came up, and her gaze collided with his. "Ah . . . it's difficult to explain."

"This class means a lot to you, doesn't it?"

Erin nodded. "One of the women has been on my mind the last couple of days. She hasn't centered herself yet, and —"

"Centered herself?"

"It's a counseling term. Basically, what it means is that she hasn't come to grips with who and what she is and needs to brace herself for whatever comes her way. Right now she's suffering from shock and emotional pain, and the smallest problem overpowers her. Frankly, I'm worried."

"Tell me about her." Brand held out his arm, wanting Erin to scoot close and rest her head on his chest. He'd been looking for a subtle, natural way of doing so without putting Erin on red alert.

He was almost surprised when she did move toward him. She didn't exactly cuddle up in his arms, but she braced her back against his chest and stretched her legs out in front of her. His arm reached across her shoulder blades.

"She's taking my class because after thirty-odd years of marriage her husband is leaving her. From what I understand there's another woman involved."

"I didn't know people would divorce after staying married for so many years. Frankly, it doesn't make a lot of sense."

"It happens," Erin explained softly, "more than you'd guess."

"Go on, I didn't mean to interrupt you. Tell me about . . ."

"I'll call her Margo. That isn't her name, of course."

Brand nodded. It felt so good to have Erin in his arms. He'd been fantasizing about it for days. The hold wasn't as intimate as he would have liked, but with this sweet Irish miss he'd need to go slowly.

"She's in her early fifties and never worked outside the home. All she knows how to be is a homemaker and a wife. I'd venture to guess that she's never written a check. I know for a fact she doesn't drive. At a time in her life when she was looking forward to retirement, she needs to find a career and make a home for herself."

"What about children? Surely, they'd stick by their mother at a time like this."

"Two daughters. They're both married and live outside the state. From what I can remember, one lives in California and the other someplace in Texas. Margo's completely alone, probably for the first time in her life."

"How's she handling it?"

"It's hard to tell. We're only two classes into the course, but as I said before, she's shaky and fragile. Time will help."

"My parents were divorced." Brand seldom spoke of his family, and even more rarely of the trauma that had ripped his life apart at such a tender age. "I was just a kid at the time."

"Was it bad?"

He answered her with a short nod. Without a doubt, it was the worst ordeal Brand could ever remember happening to him. His whole world had been shattered. He'd become a weapon to be used against one parent or the other. And he'd only been eleven at the time. Far too young to understand, far too old to cry.

"I rarely saw my father afterward. Every time he and my mother were in the same room together, they'd start arguing. My guess is that it was easier for him to move as far away as possible than to deal with her."

"So when he divorced your mother, he divorced you, too?"

Once again, Brand responded with a short nod. His life had been filled with one trauma after another after his father had moved out of the state. A year or two later, when his mother had remarried, all communication and child support had stopped. Brand had been made to feel guilty for every bit of food he ate or each pair of shoes he outgrew. While attending college, he'd become involved in the officers' training program offered by the navy. His life had changed from that moment forward. For the better.

Brand found security and acceptance in the navy. What the military had given him, it had taken away from Erin. He understood her complaints well. She hated moving, never planting roots or building lasting relationships. Brand thrived on the security. The navy was his home. The navy was his life. No one would ever take that away from him. There would always be a navy. Budget cuts hurt, bases were being closed down all across the country and military spending was being decreased, but he was secure, more secure than he had been since childhood.

"But I have a feeling about Margo," Erin continued. "She's far stronger than she realizes. That knowledge will come in time, but she may travel some rough waters before this ordeal is finished."

"You're strong, too."

Erin leaned her head to examine his face, and Brand took advantage of the moment to press his hands gently to her rosy cheeks. Her eyes found his, and he read her confusion as clearly as he viewed her eagerness. She wanted this kiss as much as he wanted to kiss her.

Gently he pressed his mouth to hers. The kiss was deep and thorough, his lips sliding across hers with unhurried ease and a familiarity that belied their experience. Slowly he lifted his head and drew in a deep, stabilizing breath. A bolt of sizzling electricity arched between them.

"Oh, damn," Erin whispered, sounding very much as if she were about to weep. Her eyes remained closed, and Brand was tempted to kiss her moist lips a second time. In fact, he had to restrain himself from doing so.

"Damn?"

"I was afraid of this." Her words were hoarse, as if she were having trouble speaking. Her eyes fluttered open, and she gazed up longingly at him. Irish eyes. Sweet Irish eyes.

"Don't be afraid," he whispered, just before he kissed her a second time. And a third. A fourth. His hands were in her hair, loving the silky feel of it as he ran his fingers through the lengthy curls.

Gradually he felt her opening up to him,

like the satin petals of a rosebud. Either she'd had poor teachers or she was inexperienced in the art of kissing. Brand didn't know which, didn't care.

Positioned as they were against the tree, he couldn't get close enough to her. The need to cradle her softness grew until every part of his body ached. He wanted her beneath him, warm and willing. Open and sweet.

With their mouths joined, he rolled away from the tree, taking her with him. Erin gave a small cry of alarm, and when she opened her mouth he groaned and thrust his tongue deep into the moist warmth.

She rebelled for a moment, not having expected this new intimacy. It took her a second to adjust before she responded, meekly at first, by giving him her tongue. They touched, stroked and played against each other in an erotic game until Brand deepened the kiss to a level neither of them would be able to tolerate for long.

Her hands clenched his shirt, and Brand wondered if she could feel how hard and fiercely his heart was beating. He could feel hers, excited and chaotic, pounding against his chest. Her pulse wasn't the only thing he could feel. Her nipples had pearled and stood out. The need to slip his hand under her sweater and fill his palm with her breast ate at him like lye. He couldn't . . . not here.

He longed to feel her and taste her. Sweet

heaven, if he didn't stop now he'd end up *really* frightening her. He probably had already. He was as hard as concrete against her thigh. The way they were lying, there wasn't any way he could hide what she was doing to him. Only years of training and self-discipline kept him still. He longed to rotate his hips to help ease the terrible ache in his loins.

He kissed Erin again, struggling within himself to take it slow and easy. His mouth gentled over hers, in sharp contrast to the wild, uncontrolled kisses they'd shared seconds earlier. She groaned and moved against him, causing Brand to moan himself. His innocent Irish miss hadn't a clue of the torment she was putting him through. Dear heaven, she was sweet. So warm and moist.

Brand had fully intended to cool their lovemaking, but he made a single tactical error that was nearly his undoing. Just because a kiss was gentle, it didn't make it any less sensual, or any less devastating.

By the time Brand lifted his head, he was weak, depleted, yet at the same time exhilarated. Shocked eyes stared up at him. He smiled and noted how the edges of her delectable mouth quivered slightly.

She raised her hand, and her fingertips grazed his face. Her touch was as smooth and light as a velvet glove. Unable to resist, Brand kissed her again.

"Are you going to say damn again?" he teased.

Her grin widened. "No."

"But you should?"

She nodded, then closed her eyes and slowly expelled her breath. "I don't know how this happened."

"You don't?"

"I'd hoped . . ."

He pressed a finger across her lips. "I know what you hoped! You couldn't have picked a more public place and for obvious reasons, which I fear have backfired on us both. As it is, I may have to lie on my belly the rest of the afternoon."

"You will?" As the meaning of his words sank into her brain, Erin's cheeks blossomed with color. "I . . . I shouldn't have said anything." As if she needed something to occupy her hands, she reached for one of the oranges, peeling it open. She held out a dripping slice to him. "Want one?"

Sitting with his legs folded in front of him, Brand nodded. He thought Erin meant to hand it to him, but instead she leaned forward to feed him personally. Her eyes were locked with his. A second slice followed the first, but when the juice flowed from the edge of his mouth she bent toward him and licked it away.

When her tongue scraped the side of his lips, Brand's heart went still. She offered him

71

another slice, but he took it from her fingers and fed it to her. He watched as she chewed and swallowed, and then he leaned forward to kiss her. She tasted of orange and woman. He deepened the kiss and was gratified when she opened up to him in excited welcome. His tongue swept her mouth in slow, even strokes, conquering as it plundered.

Erin looped her arms around his neck and melted in his arms. "I promised myself this wouldn't happen."

"And now that it has?" He angled his head to one side and dropped a series of long, slow kisses on her neck, working his way under her chin and to her ear. "Do you want me to stop?"

"No."

The satisfaction that one word gave him was worth a thousand from anyone else. "Let's get out of here."

"Why?" How afraid she sounded.

His mouth hovered a scant inch from hers. "Because there are other places I want to kiss you, and I don't think you'd appreciate me doing so in public."

His lips inched back to hers in breath-stealing increments. The closer his mouth edged toward hers, the choppier her breath became.

"Brand . . . I don't think this is such a good —"

He silenced any protest with a hot, need-filled kiss. She welcomed his tongue, and was panting by the time he dragged his mouth from hers.

"Come on," he said, vaulting to his feet. He reached for her hand, pulling her upright. "Let's get out of here."

"Where . . . will we go?"

"Your place."

"Brand . . . I don't know."

He turned and planted his hands squarely on her shoulders, his eyes refusing to release hers. "I'm not going to make love to you, yet. That's a promise. We need to talk, and when we do, I want it to be in private."

She might have had objections to the high-handed manner in which he was issuing orders, but she didn't voice any. Nor did she speak while he drove to her house in West Seattle, although the ride took nearly thirty minutes. The only words she did manage were to relay her address and give directions once he was in the vicinity.

It wasn't until he helped her out of the car that she did chance a look in his direction. Brand had to smile. Her eyes seemed so round and wide, an aircraft carrier could have sailed through them.

"He said *yet*, you idiot." She repeated the sentence two or three times once they were inside the house. Brand found it amusing the way she talked to herself. Without telling him what she was doing, she walked, as if in a daze, into the kitchen and started assembling a pot of coffee.

Brand hadn't a clue what she was mumbling about. He wasn't interested in coffee, either, but since she hadn't asked him, he didn't say so.

"There's something you should know," he began. Then he changed his mind. This wasn't the time. He needed to taste her again.

"What?" She sounded as though she were coming out of a coma.

"Come here first."

She walked over to him as though she were sleepwalking, her steps sluggish and her look disoriented.

"Kiss me first," Brand whispered, "then I'll tell you."

As if she were in a stupor, she planted her hands on his chest, then stood on tiptoe and brushed her lips lightly over his. Unable to hold himself back any longer, Brand wrapped his arms around her, pulled her close and buried his face in her neck, savoring her softness.

For the last several days he'd been wondering what it was about Erin that preyed so heavily on his mind. After kissing her, he understood. He felt strong when he was with her. Strong emotionally. Strong physically. When they were together, he became another Samson. She gave him a feeling of being needed.

She needed him, too. She'd never admit it, of course, never deliberately tell him as much, but it was true.

"You said we needed to talk," she reminded him. With what seemed like a good deal of effort, she moved away from him.

"Yes," Brand answered softly, and rubbed a hand along the back of his neck. "What are you doing every day for the next four days?"

"Why?" A worried look dominated her face. Then her eyes, which had been so gentle and submissive only seconds before, flashed to life with a fire that all but scorched Brand. "You don't need to tell me. You're only going to be in Seattle four more days."

Chapter Four

"Why are you so angry?" Brand demanded, not understanding Erin. He was being as honest as he knew how to be with her, and she was looking at him as though he'd just announced he was an ax murderer.

"You know . . . You know . . ." She walked over to the cupboard and slammed two ceramic mugs down with enough force to crack the kitchen counter. "From the beginning you've known how I feel about navy men."

"I didn't mislead you," he reminded her in as reasonable a tone as he could muster. "You knew from the first I was on a short assignment."

Grudgingly she answered him with an abrupt nod.

If Brand was upset about anything, it was the fact that he'd waited so long to do as his friend Casey MacNamera had asked and checked up on the old man's daughter. If Brand had contacted her the first week he'd arrived in Seattle, a lot of things might have worked out differently.

"Here's your coffee." The hot liquid sloshed over the edges of the mug when Erin set it on the glass table top.

He pulled out a beige cushioned chair and

sat. His hands cupped the mug while he waited, giving Erin the time she needed to sort through her feelings.

It took her far longer than he expected. She paced the kitchen ten or fifteen times, pausing twice, her eyes revealing her confusion and her doubt. Both times she glared at him as though he'd committed unspeakable crimes. After a while, her brisk steps slowed, and she started talking to herself, mumbling something unintelligible.

"Am I forgiven?" Brand asked when she sat in the chair across the table from him.

"Sure," she answered, giving him a weak smile. "What's there to forgive?"

"I'm pleased you feel that way." Because of the abrupt switch in her behavior, Brand didn't feel as confident.

"Meeting you has . . . been an interesting experience" was all she'd say.

Brand felt the same way himself. "Can I see you tomorrow?"

"I'm busy."

Brand frowned, and a sinking sensation attacked the pit of his stomach. "Doing what?"

"I don't believe that's any of your concern."

Oh, boy, here it comes, he mused. "But it is. If you're attending church services, then I'll go with you. If you've promised a friend you'd help them move, then I'll cart boxes myself." If Erin thought the Irish could be stubborn, she had yet to butt heads with the German in him.

"Brand, please don't make this any more difficult than it already is. I can't change who I am for you. I told you from the first I don't want to become involved with anyone in the military, and I meant it. I don't know why you can't accept that. And I don't even want to know. You're leaving, and when it comes right down to it, I'm glad. It's for the best."

"I'm stationed in Hawaii. It's not all that —"

"I have no intention of flying off to the islands for an occasional weekend, nor can I afford to, so don't even suggest it."

"The only thing I was going to suggest was the two of us getting to know each other better." He strove to sound casual, although there wasn't a single bone in his entire body that was indifferent to Erin. She affected him far more strongly than any other woman he'd ever known. Generally he was the one seeking an out in the relationship.

Erin sipped her coffee, more relaxed now. *Centered* was the term she'd used earlier, and he could see it in her. She'd made her decision, and neither hell nor high water would sway her from it.

"Will you see me again?" He didn't like asking a second time. It went against his pride, but he was learning that when it came to Erin MacNamera he was willing to give more than with anyone else.

Her nod took a long time coming, but when it did, Brand felt the tension ease.

"On one condition," she added.

"Name it."

Her beautiful dark eyes found his, and he noted how lost and bewildered she looked. "What is it?"

"No more . . . of what happened today in the park."

"You don't want me to kiss you again?" Brand was sure he'd misunderstood her. They were just beginning to know each other, learn about each other, and it seemed ridiculous for them to put their relationship into a holding pattern now.

"I'm offering you my friendship, Brand, nothing more." He wanted Erin for more than a friend, but saying so would likely cut off any chance he had with her. If those were the ground rules she was setting, then far be it for him to argue with her. He fully intended to do whatever he could to change her mind, but she'd learn that soon enough.

"All right," he said, grinning at her. "We'll be friends."

"No more of that, either," she countered sharply.

"What?" Brand hadn't a clue what she was talking about.

"That smile. The navy could launch missiles with that smile of yours."

Was that a fact? Brand mused. He'd have to remember that and use it often.

Agreeing to this dinner date wasn't one of her most brilliant moves, Erin decided later. Brand was scheduled to fly out of the Whidbey Island Naval Station early the following morning. They'd talked several times by phone, but she hadn't seen Brand since their date on Saturday afternoon.

Erin hated admitting what a good time she'd had with the lieutenant j.g. They'd toured Sand Point and had a picnic at Woodland Park Zoo, although the only animal she'd encountered was of the human variety. And something else had happened Saturday, something she kept trying to forget and couldn't.

Brand had kissed her senseless.

It caused her cheeks to burn every time she thought about the way she'd abandoned herself in his arms. No one had ever told her kissing could be so wonderful . . . especially the way Brand was doing it. She felt achy and restless every time she dwelled on it. Her heart would start to beat, slow and sluggish, and the heat would start creeping through her. A warm excitement would fill her, and she could find no way of explaining it. The heat started low in her abdomen and grew into an achy restlessness that disturbed her beyond anything she'd ever experienced.

Then her breasts would start throbbing the way they had when he'd pressed her against the blanket and whispered there were other places he longed to kiss her, too. It had been all she could do not to ask him to take her nipples in his mouth . . . She wished he had — which was a crazy idea, since they'd been in a public place.

It wouldn't have stopped there. Erin knew that as well as she knew her own name.

Brand awoke carnal instincts in her. She'd never guessed she was capable of feeling sensual sensations as strong as this. Erin had always assumed she knew herself well. Apparently that wasn't the case after all. Not if Brand could evoke such an overwhelming reaction in her with a series of wet kisses.

The doorbell chimed, and, inhaling softly, she braced herself, walked across the living room and opened the front door to Brand.

"Hi." His gaze gave her an appreciative sweep. "Are you ready?"

She nodded. Damn, it was good to see him again. She hated to admit that much, and she gave herself a quick mental shake. Somehow, someway, she was going to get through this evening, and once she did it would be over between them. He could go his way and she could go hers, and never the twain would meet.

Once they were in the car, Erin suggested a Mexican restaurant that was less than a mile from her house. The food was good and cheap. All Erin was looking to do was to survive this evening with her heart intact.

The walls of the El Lindo were made of white stucco and decorated with several huge sombreros in bright shades of turquoise and gold. Erin studied the pictures on the wall, which were displayed in wide, bulky frames, in an effort to avoid looking at Brand. She dared not allow her eyes to meet his for fear of reviving memories from their last encounter.

"So where are you headed to next?" she asked, making sure her voice contained just the right amount of friendliness. A tortilla chip commanded her full attention as she dipped it in salsa.

"Probably San Francisco."

"When?" It felt good to have the upper hand in the conversation, Erin mused.

"Soon. A month or two from now, maybe less. Have you been there?"

"I don't think there are more than a handful of naval bases where I *haven't* been." She made light of the fact, when in reality it was a source of fierce bitterness. The comment was made with just enough sarcasm for Brand to recognize she wouldn't return to that lifestyle again for anything or anyone in the world, including him. He must have gotten the message, because his face tightened into a frown.

Erin ordered the cheese-and-onion enchiladas, her favorite, and Brand asked for the chili verde. Both dinners were excellent, and they lingered over coffee, talking about a variety of bland but safe subjects. Brand told her about his two best friends, Alex Romano and Catherine Fredrickson. Like him, Alex was a surface warfare officer. Catherine was an attorney. All three had been stationed in Hawaii for four years.

When Brand pulled into the driveway in front of her house, her hand was already on the handle. She had a farewell, so-glad-we-had-this-chance-to-meet talk all prepared, but she wasn't allowed to say one word of it.

Brand reached across the seat and gripped her hand. "Invite me in for coffee."

"We just finished having a cup."

"Invite me in anyway."

"I . . . don't know if that's such a good idea."

"Yes, it is. Trust me."

"All right." But she wasn't pleased about it.

She led the way into her compact home. Buying a house was one of the first things she'd done after being hired for the Community Action Program. The payments were high, but Erin didn't mind the sacrifice, because for the first time in her life she didn't have to worry about being forced to move. No one was going to casually announce it was time to relocate. She didn't need to worry that everything she owned was going to be stripped away from her almost overnight.

For the first time in her life, she was planting roots. They weren't as deep as she wanted, not yet, but she intended for them to be. This home was hers and hers alone. It was her security, her defense, her shelter. Falling crazy in love with a navy man would threaten everything she'd strived to build for herself in the past several years, and she adamantly refused to allow it to happen.

Once they were inside, Erin turned on the lights and pointed to the bulky stuffed chair angled in front of the television. "Make yourself comfortable. Would you like some coffee?"

"Please."

Brand followed her into the kitchen. "We've avoided the subject all evening," he said, standing directly behind her. He wasn't actually pinning her against the counter, but he made it plain he could if he wanted to.

"We don't need to talk about it."

"We do," he countered swiftly. "I'm leaving. Trust me, I don't want to go, but I am. It's part of my job. I don't know when I'll be back, but I will be."

She tried to look as uninterested as she could. "Look me up when you do," she said flippantly.

Brand frowned anew. "Erin MacNamera, that wasn't nice."

"I apologize." She didn't completely understand what she'd said that was so wrong. If Brand thought she was going to sit around moping for him, he was dead wrong.

Yes, she enjoyed his company, and when he left she'd miss him for a while, but after a week or so she wouldn't give him more than the occasional fleeting thought.

"Kiss me," Brand instructed.

Erin's heart went still. She'd prefer leaping off the Tacoma Narrows Bridge to granting Brand Davis the privileges she had the day of their picnic. He might as well ask her to light a stick of dynamite and wave it around for everyone to see what a fool she was.

She tried to break away from him. "I can't . . . I have no intention of kissing you."

"Just once, to say goodbye."

"Brand . . ."

His hands drifted up and down her lifeless arms, bringing her against him. Erin didn't know who moved, him or her.

"If you won't kiss me, then you leave me no choice but to kiss you." He angled his head to one side and placed his moist, hot mouth over hers.

The kiss was unbearably good; it was all Erin could do not to melt at his feet. Somehow she managed to stand stiff and straight, not granting him an inch.

Brand appeared unconcerned by her lack of response. He drew her wrists up and placed her hands around his neck, then locked his own arms tight around her waist, lifting her against him.

Erin didn't want to respond, had promised herself she wouldn't, but before she knew what was happening her lips had parted and her tongue was eagerly searching out his. If only he weren't so gentle. So tender and generous. Erin felt as if she were drowning in sheer ecstasy. She moaned, and the sound seemed to encourage Brand all the more.

He kissed her again and again, and it was even better than his lovemaking had been in the park. Even more wonderful, and she hadn't thought that was possible. Brand's kisses were long and deep, and before she knew it Erin was clinging to him mindlessly.

He released her slowly, letting her slide down his front. Once her feet were firmly planted on the floor, his hand closed over her breast. Erin whimpered — it was a soft sound of pleasure — as he battled with the buttons of her silk blouse, peeling it open. He unfastened her bra and filled his palms with her lush fullness. His sigh went through her like a spear, and as hard as she tried, she couldn't keep from reacting.

Her nipples were so hard, they burned and throbbed and ached in a way she'd never experienced until now. Her hands were in

Brand's hair and her head was thrown back as she squirmed against him. She wanted his mouth on her breasts, just the way she'd imagined. Just the way she'd dreamed about for the past two nights.

As if reading her thoughts, Brand gave her what she yearned to experience, drawing her nipple into his moist, warm mouth and sucking lightly, then strongly, then lightly again. A sensation of pleasure so hot it bordered on pain flashed through her like lightning. It was all Erin could do to hold still. If he continued this much longer, she'd be climbing the walls. Literally.

The sensation was incredible, beyond description. She wanted him, needed him. Soon her own fingers were busy. She was so impatient, she nearly ripped the buttons off his shirt. It became imperative that she do to him what he was doing to her. She didn't know if this was something women did to men, but she longed to return the pleasure he was giving her.

With her arms wrapped securely around his neck, she nuzzled the hollow at his throat, sliding her tongue back and forth in lazy circles while she fiddled with the opening on his shirt. Once it was free, she spread it back from his shoulders.

Erin had never seen a man as close to perfect as Brand. He was stronger than anyone she'd ever known. And he smelled so good, of spice and bay rum. He'd probably sprayed himself with an aphrodisiac before meeting her for dinner, but Erin was beyond the point of caring.

Brand's muscular body felt hot to the touch. She was unable to keep her hands still. They roamed up and down the sides of his waist, then over the lightly haired planes of his broad chest until she inadvertently touched the tight buds of his nipples. When she did, she was gratified by the shudder that went through him, starting with a rippling motion in his massive shoulders and working its way down.

"Erin," he pleaded, "no more."

She ignored him. After all, he ignored her, and fair was fair. Her mouth fastened over the tight pearl of his nipple, and she gave him the same treatment he had given her. He tasted as wonderful as he smelled.

"Erin," he pleaded a second time. She paused long enough to sigh, loving the sound of his voice, so low and husky. It spurred her on more powerfully than any words he might have said.

"We've got to stop before it's too late," he warned, working his hands between them.

Her response was to curl her fingers more tightly in the hair on his chest and tug lightly.

"Erin."

This time something in his voice did capture her attention. His hands were on her shoulders, and he heaved a giant breath as he wrapped his arms around her waist. Erin buried her face in his neck, embarrassed by the things she'd done and allowed him to do.

She rarely cried, but she felt the salty wetness coat her cheeks.

"Casey would shoot me dead if he knew how close I've come to making love to you."

Erin abruptly broke away from him, her eyes clouded with confusion. She nearly stumbled, finding herself off balance. Nevertheless, she glared up at Brand. "How did you know my father's name is Casey?"

Brand closed his eyes slowly, as if he'd inadvertently allowed a top government secret to pass from his lips. "That's a long story."

Erin jerked away and turned her back to him while her fingers frantically worked to assemble her bra and blouse. Her hands were trembling so badly, it made the task nearly impossible. When she'd finished, she walked across the room and removed her mug from the table, simply because she needed something to cling to. She felt as if she were being beaten by an invisible force, shaken so hard her teeth were rattling.

"How do you know my father?" she demanded a second time, and her voice trembled as severely as her fingers.

"We're friends. We worked together a few years back, hit it off, and have kept in touch ever since," Brand announced, looking none too pleased. If anything, he looked downright irritated. "When Casey learned I was flying into Seattle for this assignment, he asked me to check up on you. Apparently he's worried that you're working too hard. Your father's a good man, Erin."

That wasn't exactly the way Erin would have described him at the moment. He was a meddling, interfering old fool who couldn't keep out of her life!

"So Dad sent you out to spy on me?" she demanded coolly.

Brand nodded reluctantly.

"When we met at the Blue Lagoon . . . it wasn't by chance?"

"Not exactly. I followed you there."

Erin closed her eyes and placed her hand over her mouth. "Dear heaven."

"I know it sounds bad."

"Bad?" she cried. "You . . . I was set up by my own father!" She started pacing, because standing still was impossible. Turning abruptly, she glared at him with eyes she was sure conveyed her feelings exactly. "What about everything else? The kissing, the . . . petting. Did Dad ask you to indoctrinate me into —"

"Erin, no." He expelled his breath sharply and jammed his fingers into his scalp with enough force to remove a fistful of hair. "Okay, I made a mistake. I should have told you the first night that your father and I are friends. If you want to condemn me for that, go ahead, I deserve it. But everything else was for real."

Erin didn't know whether she believed him or not, but at this point it didn't matter. She crossed her arms and glared at the ceiling, trying fruitlessly to gather her thoughts and make sense of what had happened between them.

"I liked you the minute I saw you," Brand admitted slowly, "and the feeling has intensified each and every day since. I don't know what's happening between us. It's crazy, but I feel . . . Hell, I don't know what I feel, other than the fact I don't want to lose you."

"That's what I can't make you understand," she cried. "You lost me the minute I realized you were navy."

"Erin . . ."

"I think you should go." The lump in her throat made it impossible for her to speak distinctly. When Brand didn't budge, she pointed the way to the door. "Please, just leave."

Brand hesitated, then nodded. "All right, I can see I've really messed this up. At the rate I'm going, I'll only make matters worse. I'll try to give you a call before I leave tomorrow."

She nodded, although she hadn't a clue what she was agreeing to.

"I've got your address."

Once more she moved her head, willing to concede anything as long as he would get out of her home, her safe haven, and leave her alone. She felt shocked as she rarely had been. Shaken and hurt. To the best of her knowledge, her father had never done anything like this before. Once she got through with him, she would damn well make sure he wouldn't again.

Brand paused at the front door. "I'm not saying goodbye to you, Erin." He stood there for the longest moment without moving. His eyes were filled with regret. It seemed that he wanted to say something more but changed his mind.

Erin looked away, not wanting to encourage him to do anything but leave her in peace. Or whatever was left of that precious commodity.

The door closed, and she glanced up to discover that Brand was gone. A breath rattled through her lungs as she continued to stare into space.

It was over. Brand Davis had left.

Brand closed his eyes as he listened to the message on Erin's answering machine for the tenth time. He was paying long-distance rates to speak to a stupid tape recorder. Not that it had done any good. Not once had she returned his call.

She hadn't even tried.

He'd contacted her every day since he'd returned to Hawaii, but he hadn't spoken to her yet. It didn't seem to matter what time of the day he phoned, she wasn't home. Or if she was, she wasn't answering.

He'd tried writing too. Brand wasn't much of a letter writer, but each night since he'd been back he had sat down faithfully and written to Erin. Not just short notes, either. Real letters, sometimes two and three pages each. He wrote about things he'd rarely shared with longtime friends. He wasn't revealing deep, dark secrets, just feelings. Feelings a man wouldn't easily convey to another human being unless that person was someone special. Erin was more than special. Until he'd left Seattle, Brand hadn't realized how important Casey's daughter had become to him.

Ten days into his letter-writing campaign, he had yet to receive so much as a postcard from her. It didn't take a master's degree for him to figure out that his sweet Irish rose had no intention of answering his letters, either.

Rarely had Brand felt more discouraged. He was frustrated enough to contact Casey MacNamera.

"Casey, you old goat, it's Brand," he said, speaking into the telephone receiver. The long-distance wire hummed between them.

Casey had retired in Pensacola, Florida.

"Well if it isn't Face Davis, himself. How you doing, boy?"

"Good. Real good." Which was only a slight exaggeration.

"I take it you told Erin about me asking you to check up on her. Good grief, that girl nearly had a conniption right on the phone. I don't think I've ever heard her more shooting mad. Nearly shouted me ears off, she did." The pot-bellied MCPO paused to chuckle, as if the whole matter were one of great amusement.

"I didn't mean to give it away," Brand said by way of apology. "We sort of hit it off . . . Erin and me." He paused, hoping Casey would make some comment either way. He didn't.

"That oldest girl of mine has got a temper on her. If you ever cross her, the best advice I can give you is to stand back and protect yourself from the fireworks."

"Speaking of Erin," Brand said, delicately leading into the purpose of this call, "how is she?"

"I can't rightly say." Casey paused and chuckled again. "She didn't get around to telling me anything about her health. She was far more concerned about giving me a solid piece of her mind."

"Did she say anything about me?"

Casey paused. "Not really. Only that she

didn't appreciate the fact I'd sent you her way."

"I appreciated it."

"You did?" Casey's voice lowered suspiciously. "What makes you say that?"

"Erin and I dated two or three times. You've done yourself proud, you old goat. Erin's a wonderful woman."

"She's not your type."

Brand was about to take offense at that. "Why isn't she?"

"I thought you liked your women sleek and sophisticated. Erin's not like that. Not in the least. The girl's meat-and-potatoes."

"I like Erin. In fact, I like her a whole lot. I hope that doesn't offend you, because I intend to see more of her."

Brand expected a long list of possible responses from Casey. It didn't include laughter, but laugh was exactly what Casey MacNamera did. In fact, he burst into loud chuckles, as if Brand had just told the funniest joke of the year.

"Good luck, Brand. You're going to need it with my Erin. That woman's stubborner than a Tennessee mule. I don't want to discourage you, but she won't have anything to do with someone in the navy."

"I plan to change her mind."

"As far as I can see, you've got a snowball's chance in hell of ever doing that. Now, before I forget it, tell me how it is you got

95

chosen for this cushy assignment. I should have known that handsome face of yours was going to get you a boondoggle one of these days. Where you headed to next?"

"San Francisco." And none too soon, as far as Brand was concerned, because the city was only six hundred miles from Seattle. And that was a hell of a lot closer than Hawaii.

"Oh, please, don't let there be another letter from Brand," Erin prayed aloud as she pulled into her driveway. For twenty days straight, she'd received a letter from him every day.

Twenty days.

She walked up to the mailbox on her porch and lifted the lid. Two flyers and a bill. There wasn't a letter.

Unreasonably disappointed, she sorted through everything again, and then stuck her hand back inside the mailbox. It was there, tucked down in the back.

Erin didn't know whether she should be upset or relieved. What did it matter? She'd been of two minds from the moment she'd met Brand Davis.

Two minds and one heart.

Opening her front door with her key, Erin walked inside her home and slapped everything down on the kitchen counter. Making herself a cup of tea, she leafed through the flyers and set the bill aside.

Once the tea was made, she reached for Brand's letter, opening it with her index finger. She counted five pages. Five long, single-spaced, handwritten pages. Wouldn't he ever stop?

"Oh, please, make him stop writing," she pleaded once more as her gaze hungrily scanned each word, canceling out her prayer.

When the first letter had arrived, Erin had righteously marched to the outside garbage can and tossed it inside. She'd refused to read a single line of what that deceiver had written. From there, she'd made herself dinner, muttering sanctimonious epithets directed at the lieutenant j.g. and then headed off to her Women in Transition class, feeling downright pious about having tossed out the letter.

The feeling hadn't lasted long.

At nine-thirty, when she'd returned from class, she'd reached for her flashlight and, without a pause, started rooting through the garbage until she found the envelope.

She'd called herself every word for fool that she could think of in the days since. As much as she hated to admit it, each night she rushed home, eager for word from Brand.

She was living in a fool's paradise. Nothing would come of this. First off, she had no intention of ever answering him.

Nor did she intend to see him again. Their

differences were irreconcilable, as far as she could discern. There were no compromises for her and Brand. He was military, and she adamantly refused to fall in love with someone in the armed services — especially someone in the navy.

Each and every time they'd been together, they'd hashed over their differences. There was no way to arbitrate this issue, no meeting in the middle. Nothing he could say would change her mind. Nothing she could say would alter his. Rehashing their differences would only be a waste of time and energy, and Erin had enough on her mind as it was.

The phone rang just as she was turning the last page of his letter. He was giving a humorous account of something he and his friend Alex had done. Without thinking, she reached for the receiver, not giving a thought to letting the recorder answer for her as had been her habit of late.

"Hello," she said softly.

"Erin? Erin, is that really you?"

It was Brand, and he sounded absolutely amazed that she'd answered the phone.

Chapter Five

"Ah . . ." Erin stammered, resisting the urge to replace the receiver and escape talking to Brand. That would be a coward's way of handling the situation. She and Brand were bound to have a showdown one time or another, and the longer she delayed the confrontation the more difficult it would be.

"Okay, just listen," Brand said, speaking with authority, his voice slightly high-pitched, his words rushed. "I've got everything I want to say all planned."

"Brand, please . . ."

"You can tell me whatever it is you want when I'm finished, okay?"

She nodded, closed her eyes, then whispered, "All right."

"You asked me once why I continued to ask you out. Do you remember that?"

"Yes." She did, all too well.

"I thought I had it figured out before I left Seattle. I liked you from the first. You're a caring, warm, generous woman, and anyone spending time with you would soon realize that. I noticed it long before the day at the zoo when you were telling me about the older woman in your class who's going through such a difficult time. You barely knew her, yet you sincerely cared about her and her problems."

"What has all this got to do with anything?"

"Just be patient. I'm coming to that."

Erin was so stiff, the muscles in her lower spine were starting to ache. She stood and pressed her hand to the small of her back and paced, walking as far as the telephone cord would stretch and then back again. She longed to rush him along, longed for this to be over as soon as possible. How painful it was, how much more difficult than she'd thought it would be.

"I realized shortly after our picnic that being with you makes me feel strong and good. Strong emotionally, strong physically. I realize that doesn't make a whole lot of sense to you right now. I'm not even sure I can explain it any better than that. Maybe later I can, but for now it isn't the most important thing." Brand paused and inhaled a single, choppy breath. He was speaking so fast that it was difficult for Erin to understand him. And the long-distance hum wasn't helping matters any.

"Brand . . ."

"Let me finish."

Erin's mind filled with enough arguments to sink a battleship. "All right." Only she wished he'd hurry so she could say what needed to be said and be finished with it.

"The last three weeks away from you have taught me some valuable lessons. I've written you every day."

She didn't need to be reminded of that. Every single message he'd mailed her was neatly stacked on her desk. She'd reread them so often, most had been committed to memory.

"Sitting down and putting my thoughts on paper has cleared up a lot of the confusion I've been feeling since I returned to Hawaii. It hit me almost immediately that . . ." He hesitated, as though he were fearful of her response. "I'm in love with you, Erin."

"In love with me?" she repeated, as though in a trance.

"I know you don't want to hear that, but I can't and won't apologize for the way I feel. For the first time in my life, I'm in love. I *thought* I was a hundred times before, but this is different. Better. Did you hear me, Erin? I love you."

Erin squeezed her eyes closed. Of all the things he had to say, all the nonsensical, absurd, foolish things . . . why, oh, why, did he have to tell her that?

"Say something," he pleaded. "Anything."

All the arguments she had lined up in her mind fell like dominoes, crashing against one another, tumbling into nothingness. She was left speechless.

"Erin, sweetheart, are you still there?"

"Yes." Her voice rose an octave above its normal range. "I'm here."

"I know it's something of a shock, blurting it out like this over the phone, but I swear to you I couldn't hold it inside another second. Haven't you noticed how I've signed my letters recently?"

She had. She'd preferred to ignore the obvious, even when it was slapping her in the face.

"A relationship won't work with us . . . We're too different."

"We'll make it work."

Just the way he said it, without leaving room for doubt, caused Erin to wonder if it was possible. Was loving someone enough to alleviate all the problems? Was it enough to gain a compromise where there wasn't one? Maybe it was, after all. Brand sounded so confident, so convinced.

Erin's hold tightened around the telephone receiver. "I don't see how."

"Erin, sweetheart . . . damn, I wish I was there right now. It's hell being so far away from you."

"You'll always be away from me." The truth was as cold and lifeless as ice water. How easy it was to forget he was navy. For a moment, just the slightest moment, she could feel herself lulled into believing a relationship was possible for them. If she allowed this false thinking to continue, he'd talk her out of everything that was important to her, everything she'd struggled to build. In the nick of time she realized what she was doing and pulled herself up short.

"I'll be away, yes," Brand argued, "but not all the time, and when we're together I'll make up for lost time."

"No."

"What do you mean, no?"

"Claiming you love me doesn't change anything." The words were easy enough to say, but she wasn't completely sure they were true. What she had to do was pretend they were and pray he didn't challenge her with a lot of questions.

"It does as far as I'm concerned."

"Brand, I'm sorry, I really am, but I can't see where discussing this is going to make a difference. You love the navy. I don't. You want to stay in the service, and I'd rather leap off a cliff naked than involve my life with anything that has to do with the military. We can talk until we're blue in the face, but it isn't going to change who or what we are."

Her words were greeted by a strained silence.

"You'd prefer to leap off a cliff *naked?*" Amusement echoed behind his words.

Perhaps it wasn't the best way to explain her feelings, but it was one of the worst things she could think of doing, although she had to admit it was nonsensical.

"Sweetheart, listen to me."

"No, please, I can't. It won't do any good. The best thing you can do for the both of us is forget we ever met. It isn't going to work, and prolonging the inevitable will only cause us both more pain."

"I love you. I can't —"

"You're not listening to me," she cried, hating the way her voice trembled. "You never have listened to me, and that's the problem."

Once more Brand was silent, and this time the lack of sound seemed to throb between them like a living thing.

"All right, Erin, I'm listening."

She drew in a tattered breath and started again. "What I'm trying to explain is the plain truth, as painful as it is to accept. It will never work between us. Neither of us can adjust our needs because we happen to be physically attracted to each other."

"I'm more than physically attracted to you."

Erin decided the best thing to do was ignore that statement. "I'm honored that you would feel as strongly about me as you apparently do. Personally, I think you're wonderful, too, but that doesn't make everything right. It just doesn't . . . even though that's what we want."

A moment passed before he spoke. "In

other words, you're saying you don't love me. Or, more appropriately phrased, you *won't* love me."

"Yes."

He used a one-word expletive that was meant to shock her, and did. "You're in love with me, Erin. You can deny it if you want, but it's the truth."

"I imagine your ego chooses to believe that. If that's the case, then all I can say is fine, believe what you want." She might have sounded as confident as a judge, but on the inside she'd rarely been more unnerved.

"Say it to me, then."

Erin closed her eyes and swallowed tightly. "Say what?"

"That you don't love me." A strained silence passed before he demanded it of her again. "Say it!"

God help her, Erin couldn't do it.

"Be sure and put enough emphasis on the words to make it believable," he advised, "because I know you're lying, if not to me, then to yourself."

"You have such colossal nerve." She tried to make her statement sound as if she were highly amused by his attitude.

"Say it," he demanded a third time.

A moment passed before she was able to do as he requested. She tried to speak once, but when she opened her mouth she felt her throat start to close up, and she aborted the effort.

"Erin?"

"All right, if you insist. I don't love you."

"Do you mean it?" he asked her softly, sounding almost amused.

If only he didn't make it so damn difficult. She was furious with him, furious enough to put an end to this torment. "Yes, I'm sure. Now kindly leave me alone."

"As you wish." His voice was incredibly low, filled with so many emotions that she couldn't identify them all. "Goodbye, my sweet Irish rose. Have a good life — I sure as hell plan to."

The line was disconnected while she stood holding on to the receiver. For the longest time Erin didn't move. She stood exactly as she was, the phone pressed to her ear, the drone of the line buzzing like angry, swarming bees around her.

The wetness that spilled onto her face came as a surprise. She raised her hand, and her fingertips smeared the moisture across the high arch of her cheek.

"I *will* have a good life," she choked out. "I promise I will."

"I hate to keep troubling you," Marilyn said, stepping up to Erin's scarred desk. The class had been dismissed for the evening, and Erin was sticking the leftover handouts inside her leather briefcase.

Over the past several weeks, Erin had been keeping close tabs on Marilyn, charting her progress. The older woman had looked something like a baked apple when she'd first come into class. Shriveled up and burdened by the weight of her problems. She'd worn the same dress and the same pair of shoes and little, if any, makeup. All that had gradually changed over the weeks. Marilyn had hired an attorney, gotten a part-time job with a department store and signed up for driving school. She walked a little taller and held her head higher. The going hadn't been easy. Subject to depression and fits of rage, she'd recently confessed to Erin that she'd destroyed one entire wall of the family home.

"It's no trouble, Marilyn. It's always good to talk to you."

"I just wanted you to know I got my driver's license this afternoon."

"Congratulations!"

Marilyn's grin went from ear to ear. "I didn't ever think I'd be able to do it, but the examiner who gave me the road test was very understanding." Excitement lit up her eyes. "I don't mind telling you, I was nervous in the beginning. I backed out of the parking space the wrong way and then went over the curb on the way out of the parking lot. I thought for sure the examiner was going to fail me, but then I got to thinking about the things you've been saying in class, and I decided to make the best of it."

"And you passed?"

"By two points. They didn't exactly throw a parade in my honor, and the examiner did talk to me two or three minutes afterward, suggesting that I take it nice and easy for a while, which I intend to do. When he told me I'd passed the test, I got so excited, I nearly kissed the man."

The picture that scene presented in Erin's mind was amusing enough to bring a smile to her lips. She hadn't been doing a lot of smiling lately. Not since her phone conversation with Brand.

Over and over she'd played back their discussion in her mind. There were better ways of handling the situation with Brand. Yet she'd accomplished what she'd set out to do. Her methods hadn't been the best, but then, she'd never handled anything like this before.

A few days after speaking to Brand for the last time, she'd sat down and written her father a letter hot enough to blister the mailman's fingers. She'd poured out her outrage, claimed he'd insulted her intelligence and her sense of pride and demanded that he stay out of her life.

In the morning she'd tossed the letter into the garbage where it belonged. Her father couldn't be blamed because she'd fallen in love with Brand Davis. As much as she'd like to fault her overprotective parent, all he'd done was ask Brand to check up on her. Everything else that had happened was strictly between her and the lieutenant j.g.

Feeling pleased for Marilyn, Erin drove back to her house, showered and readied for bed. She hadn't eaten anything before class, and an inspection of the freezer disclosed one frozen Salisbury steak entrée with sick-looking watery mashed potatoes and cubed carrots. The entrée looked as though it might have been left by the previous owner of the house.

Unable to shake the melancholy feeling, Erin hadn't taken the time to buy groceries that weekend. And she didn't want to traipse into the local grocery store in her flannel nightgown at this late hour.

It was either the entrée or a can of lima beans.

"Why would you buy lima beans?" she asked herself aloud. "You don't even like them."

The habit of talking to herself was becoming more pronounced, she noted, wondering what she should do about it, if anything.

Standing in front of the microwave in her bare feet, her hair wet and glistening from her shower, Erin watched the digital numbers count down. The smell of the Salisbury steak wasn't proving to be all that promising.

The timer on the microwave dinged at the same time as the doorbell chimed. It took Erin a second to realize the direction of the second bell. Her gaze swiveled from the microwave to the front door and then back again while her mind raced.

No one she knew would be visiting this time of night. But then, it wasn't likely that a burglar would announce himself, either.

Walking barefoot across the carpet, she squinted and peered out the peephole to find an eye from the other side looking back at her. She leaped back and placed her hand over her heart. She'd have recognized that eye anywhere.

Brand.

"Come on, Erin, open up. I'm in no mood to be left standing on your porch."

Pulling back the dead bolt, Erin yanked open the door. She held on to the knob and resisted the urge to launch herself straight into his arms. That fact alone answered every question she'd been taunting herself with the last two days.

Brand walked inside and set down his bag. He looked like hell. Worse. As if he'd been dragged under a car or forced to sleep in an upright position for three nights straight. A two-day beard darkened his face, and his eyes were bloodshot.

"What's that god-awful smell?" he demanded.

"My dinner." She couldn't keep from staring at him. Even though she'd never seen him look worse, he was still the most incredibly handsome man she'd ever seen in her life. Incredibly wonderful, too.

"What are you doing eating dinner this late?"

"What time is it?"

"Hell, I don't know. I just spent the last twenty hours on every conceivable means of transportation you can name. For all I know, it could be noon sometime in July."

"It's April."

"Fool's Day, no doubt."

"No." As hard as she tried, she couldn't stop staring at him. Even now, while they were carrying on a two-way conversation, she couldn't be entirely sure it was really him and not some figment of her imagination. She resisted the urge to reach out and touch him, which was even more powerful than the need to be in his arms.

"What are you doing here?"

His eyes met hers. "I don't know anymore. I asked myself that same question about the time I was on my third means of military transport."

"How long is your pass for?"

"Four days, but to be honest, I don't know how much of that time is left. Maybe I should just say what I want to say and be done with it, then get the hell out of here."

"Do you want something to eat?" That she should offer him anything was something of a joke, considering that she was warming a prehistoric frozen entrée for herself.

"Not if you're planning on serving the same thing you're eating. It smells like . . ." He left the rest unsaid, because it was apparent what he meant.

"I'll order a pizza." Somehow that made perfect sense to Erin. The fact that he was with her, standing inside her home, didn't, but she hadn't figured out a way to deal with that just yet.

"I think I should sit down," Brand announced unexpectedly. He walked across her carpet and lowered himself onto the sofa, which was against the outside wall. Then he paused and looked around, as if he couldn't quite believe he was with her.

"I'll just be a minute," she said, walking backward, thinking he might vanish if she took her eyes away from him. The flyer she'd received in the mail a few days earlier from a national pizza chain was pinned to her bulletin board along with the discount coupon. With that in hand, she punched out the phone number and ordered a delux pepperoni pizza.

By the time she returned to the living room, Brand was sound asleep on her sofa.

Brand woke not knowing where he was. He

sat bolt upright, kicking aside several blankets, and glanced around him. He still didn't know. The feeling was an eerie one.

Exhausted, he rubbed a hand down his face and gave his eyes time to adjust to the thick darkness, then slowly, thoughtfully, reviewed what he did remember.

In a flash it came to him. He was at Erin's house.

Erin. If anyone had told him even two months ago that he'd go through so many trials to get to a woman, he would have sworn they were nuts. If he'd ever doubted his love for her, making it from Hawaii to Seattle by way of Japan and Alaska proved otherwise.

And for what? He wasn't going to be able to talk any sense into her. Nothing had worked yet, but that wasn't going to stop him. Casey had claimed she was as stubborn as a Tennessee mule, and the old man was right.

But, damn it all, Brand couldn't turn his back on love and simply walk away. The way he figured it, he had only one chance with her, and that was face-to-face.

Standing, he turned on a couple of lights and noted the time. Five a.m. He found his suitcase and showered.

By the time Erin stirred, he had a pot of coffee brewed.

"Good morning," she said, standing in the

doorway. She raised the back of her hand to her mouth and yawned loudly. "There's some leftover pizza in the refrigerator if you're hungry."

"You should have woke me."

"What makes you think I didn't try."

"I wouldn't wake up?"

"The entire Third Infantry couldn't have stirred you."

He felt a bit sheepish about that. "I'm sorry. I didn't mean to crash at your place."

"Don't worry about it. If nothing else, you've given my neighbors a reason to introduce themselves." Yawning once more, she made her way into the bathroom.

It was difficult for Brand to keep his eyes off her. She was disheveled and warm from her bed. Without the least bit of trouble, his imagination kicked into gear. It was much too easy to picture himself in bed with Erin. He could feel her cuddled up against him, her warm, pale skin caressing his. He would put his hands on her breasts and lift them so that they filled his palms. Her nipples would tighten even before he could graze them with his thumbs.

Brand's breath became quick and shallow, and he half closed his eyes, savoring the fantasy. Desire throbbed through him, tightening the muscles of his thighs and his abdomen.

He felt a deep, almost painful sense of yearning for her. Not a physical need. Hell,

114

what was he thinking? Yes, he did need her physically. He'd never wanted a woman as bad as he did Erin. But what he was experiencing now was a higher plane of yearning, a profound longing. An emotional, spiritual craving he'd never understood fully until this moment. It troubled him, knowing how much was at stake in this brief time with Erin.

A few minutes later, she returned to the kitchen, dressed in a dark blue business suit. The skirt was straight and emphasized her long legs and the rounded curves of her hips and buttocks. The jacket was tailored, and the shoulders were padded. Brand poured her a cup of coffee in an effort to break the spell she had over him.

"Thanks," she whispered, pulled out a chair and sat down.

"I suppose you're wondering what I'm doing here?" he asked, realizing he sounded defensive. He was treading on thin ice with Erin, and he knew it. One wrong word and he could lose her, and that was what Brand feared most.

"I can't help wondering why you came." She braced her elbows against the glass tabletop and poised the mug of steaming coffee in front of her lips.

Brand fully intended to answer her, launch into his campaign of reason, but for the life of him he couldn't take his eyes off her mouth. Those sweet, delectable lips of hers were driving him insane.

"Would you mind if I kiss you first?"

She lowered her head so fast it was amazing her chin didn't collide with her coffee mug. "I don't think that would be a good idea."

"Why not?" he questioned softly. He pulled out the chair next to her, twisted it around and straddled it.

"You know why," she countered swiftly.

His sweet Irish rose looked so professional and imperturbable that it was enough to challenge any red-blooded male. He couldn't help himself. He pressed his index finger under her chin and raised her gaze to his. Then he leaned forward slightly and gently brushed his mouth over hers.

She released a soft sigh, and when Brand moved back he noted that her eyes remained closed and her mouth was moist and ready for further exploration.

Brand was willing, more than willing to comply.

He took her mouth again, applying a subtle pressure. He heard her coffee mug hit the table, but if it spilled or not he didn't know. Erin moaned and parted her lips for him, inviting the investigation of his tongue.

It was amazing, Brand thought, that they could be so intimate while sitting in chairs and leaning toward each other.

Her hands were braced against his shoulders and his were in her hair as he slowly rotated his mouth over hers, molding her lips with his, deepening and demanding even more from her.

Erin didn't disappoint him. She'd learned her lessons well.

Somehow Brand managed to get them into an upright position. Her arms locked around his neck, and she was squirming against him in the most tantalizing way, with a hunger that matched his own. Brand groaned, tormented by a heavy load of frustration.

Brand didn't know what he'd expected when they started, certainly not this fire that threatened to consume him. He'd felt rock-hard and aching from the moment their lips had met, and the pressure wasn't getting any better, only worse.

When he couldn't tolerate it any longer, Brand jerked his head back and battled for control. After dragging several deep breaths through his lungs, he bent forward and pressed his forehead to hers.

"I . . . I told you that kissing wasn't a good idea," she reminded him in a husky whisper. "Now you know why."

"I knew it before, but that didn't stop me." He smiled to himself as he opened his eyes enough to study her. Hungry desire was on her face. Her eyes, her nose and her delicate chin all seemed pronounced with it. Her carefully styled hair was tousled from his roving fingers, and her pink lips were the color of rose petals moist from the dew.

Her arms remained fastened around his neck, her fingers buried in his nape. Neither of them seemed capable of movement, which suited Brand just fine. He'd dreamed about holding Erin just like this a thousand times since he'd left.

"Call the office and tell them you need the day off," he told her. "Make any excuse you want, but spend the day with me."

She nodded, her eyes closed. "Aimee's furious with me."

"Why?" He couldn't resist the temptation to kiss the very tip of her nose.

"She thinks I'm a fool to let you go."

"Luckily, I didn't believe you. You do love me, don't you, Erin MacNamera?"

She took a long time answering, much longer than he deemed it should take to admit the truth.

"I shouldn't have anything to do with you."

"But you will." He made it sound as much like a command as he dared.

"I don't know," she sobbed, and her soft, slender body shook. "I just don't know. I can't believe how much I've missed you since you've been gone. I . . . I thought I could put you out of my mind, and then you started sending me those beautiful letters. Every night there was one waiting for me. I prayed and prayed that you'd get discouraged when I didn't answer. Yet I'd hurry home every night and be so grateful to hear from you again."

It might have been a little egotistical on his part, but Brand was damn proud of those letters.

"Tell me you love me, Erin," he urged, bringing her back into the shelter of his arms. "Let me hear you say it. I need that."

She bent her head against his throat and began to cry softly. "I do love you, so damn much. And you're navy."

"It could be worse," he whispered close to her ear. He'd never loved her more than he did at this moment.

He cradled her until she sniffed and gently broke away from him. "We'll spend the day together?" Her eyes avoided his.

"All day."

"Good." She smiled up at him shyly, then started to unfasten her suit jacket. Brand didn't fully comprehend what she was doing until she pulled the white silk blouse free of her waistband.

"Erin?" His voice shook noticeably. "You're undressing."

"I know." She still wouldn't look him in the eye.

His Adam's apple worked up and down his throat a couple of times. "Is there a particular reason why?"

"Yes."

It seemed every muscle in his body went tense at the same moment. She wanted to make love. He wasn't going to argue with her: good grief, he'd been thinking about the same thing from the moment she'd walked out in her flannel nightgown, all tousled and sweet this morning.

"You're sure?" He had to ask! A man shouldn't question a woman's willingness, even though he fully suspected Erin was a virgin.

"I'm s-sure."

The ache in his loins intensified.

"I . . . didn't know men questioned a woman about this sort of thing." Her voice quivered slightly.

"Normally . . . they don't, but there are certain factors we need to decide."

"Can't we do that later?" The zipper in the back of her skirt made a snakelike sound as she glided it open. She slipped the straight skirt over her hips and let it drop to her feet. Then she carefully lifted it from the floor and folded it over the back of the chair.

"You want to talk later?" he repeated. If she removed her teddy, there wouldn't be time to wait for anything. She resembled a goddess, her skin so pale it was translucent, so creamy and white. He couldn't resist her. Hell, he didn't even know why he was putting forth the effort. This was the woman he planned to love for the remainder of his life. The woman who would mother his children.

"You'll go slowly?" she asked, her voice liquid and warm.

Brand tenderly brought her into his arms. "Yes, we'll go slow, real slow. Are you sure you don't want to wait?"

"For what?"

"For us to marry." The way he figured it, they could have everything arranged within a month or so.

"Married?" Erin cried. "I — I never said anything about the two of us getting married."

Chapter Six

Erin couldn't have shocked Brand more had she announced she was an alien from Mars. "I . . . thought, I . . . assumed we'd . . . you know." The last time Brand had stammered like this had been in the third grade. He couldn't seem to get the words past his tongue without twisting and misshaping them.

"I'd assumed . . . you wanted to make love." Erin's cheeks were a shiny fire-engine red.

"I do." He couldn't argue with her over that point. He'd been half out of his mind with wanting her from the day they'd gone to the zoo. These lengthy weeks apart had intensified the longing.

"If you want to make love, then why are we standing here arguing with me over a silly thing like us being married?" She folded her arms around her middle and rooted her gaze on everything in the kitchen but him.

"We're not arguing." At least not yet. It took Brand a few more minutes to gather his wits. In an effort to do so, he had to look away from Erin. Having her this close, and this willing, was temptation enough. He couldn't glance her way and not ache inside.

His hands longed to touch her, hold her, give her everything she was asking for and more.

Her head was bowed, and the way she was standing with her arms shielding her waist brought out every protective instinct Brand possessed.

"If we're not arguing, then why are we . . . you know — waiting?"

Brand was asking himself the same question. Oh, hell, who did he think he was kidding? He wanted her. One sample of her willingness wasn't nearly enough to satisfy him. She was so damned beautiful, standing in the middle of the kitchen in her teddy, her skin so pale and baby soft. There were so many places yet to taste her and caress her, so much to teach her and for her to teach him.

The physical frustration was growing more painful, and try as he might, Brand couldn't get the picture of what she was offering him out of his mind.

He yearned to fill his palms with the lush heaviness of her breasts and take her nipples into his mouth and have her nourish him in ways he had yet to fully appreciate or understand. He wanted her legs wrapped tight around his waist and to bury himself so deep in her moist heat that he'd reach all the way to her soul. He yearned for all of those things with a hunger that was threatening to consume him, and in that instant he knew he couldn't have them.

"Get dressed, Erin."

Shocked, she blinked, and he recognized the flash of pain as it lit her beautiful brown eyes.

"Why?" she demanded.

"I believe we have a stalemate here, my dear." He strove to sound unaffected, casual, but it was a front, and a fragile one at that.

"Do you mean to tell me you refuse to make love to me simply because I'm not ready to marry you?"

"Not exactly. We're not ready to make love — not when there's so much left unresolved between us." If she didn't hurry and do as he asked and get dressed, she just might learn how precariously weak his principles actually were.

"Wh-what do you mean?" She reached for her blouse, and Brand swallowed a tight sigh of relief. He was already beginning to question his decision. He'd hurt her, shamed her for making herself vulnerable to him, and that was the last thing he'd meant to do. Hell, he thought he was being virtuous and noble.

He brought her into the circle of his arms and drew his fingers through her hair. "I didn't mean to embarrass you," he whispered. "I love you, Erin."

"You're a — a wart on a woman's pride."

He struggled to hide a grin, not daring to

let her know he was amused. "You're right," he agreed.

"Any other man would have been glad to make love to me."

"I'd be glad, too."

"Then why aren't you?"

Brand didn't know how to explain to her what he found so confusing himself. He wanted her. Needed her. Craved her. There didn't seem to be any answers to the questions that plagued him.

Holding her certainly wasn't helping matters any. The peaks of her soft breasts were pressing into his chest, and their rich abundance felt soft and swollen. Every time she breathed, her chest would nuzzle his and he'd experience an added degree of torment. She must know what she was doing to him, because she seemed to be breathing so hard and so often.

Unable to stop himself, he kissed her throat, pushing back her hair and twisting the length around his fist. Erin moaned softly. She removed her arms from around his waist, rotated her shoulders back and forth a couple of times, and before Brand realized what she'd done, her blouse lay on the floor.

"Kiss me there," she pleaded softly in a siren's voice. He was a sailor and he knew he should know better, but when she beckoned, he felt powerless to resist.

"There," she repeated.

She didn't need to explain where she meant. Brand knew. He found her breasts through the silk teddy, his tongue lapping the excited peak, drawing it into his mouth and sucking gently. Erin arched and whimpered, and when she did, her hips rubbed against the hot swell of his manhood.

Brand groaned and lost himself in her body, thoughtlessly throwing his concern and fears into a forty-knot wind. The delicious heat of desire was the only direction he needed. Slowly he slid his hand past her waistband and into the silky crevice between her thighs.

His thumb caressed the dewy mound until she softly cried out and arched upward, silently begging for what her virgin mind had yet to grasp. His finger located the apex of her femininity and slipped inside the folded layers of her heat.

She was hot and moist, and Brand groaned, or at least he thought he did. Maybe it was Erin. Perhaps both of them. It didn't matter. What did matter was the way she closed her legs convulsively around his invading hand, her hips jerking awkwardly in abruptly, frantic movements. Brand calmed her with a few whispered words of instruction then moved his hand, slowly at first, not wanting to injure or frighten her.

"Brand?" His name was a husky question on her lips.

"It's all right, sweetheart," he assured her. "It only gets better after this."

His finger slid smoothly through the moist heat as she gently rolled and swayed her hips, seeking her own satisfaction. Lightly he pushed and explored, going deeper and deeper, again and again. In and out, in an age-old rhythm.

Her hands tightened into a painful grip at his shoulders. Her long nails dug into his flesh as she arched and, with a strangled moan, tossed back her head and panted, cried out as release exploded within her.

There was no such deliverance for Brand, however, and his body throbbed with frustration and denial. He held her for several moments more until her breathing had calmed. Then he broke away from her, walked over to the sink and braced his hands against the edge as he drew in deep, even breaths.

"Brand?" Erin's silky smooth voice reached out to him. "Thank you . . . I never knew . . . I've never done anything like that with a man. I've never . . ."

His smile was weak at best, and when he spoke, his voice was husky and low. "I know."

"You did?"

He nodded.

"Can I do anything like that . . . for you?"

Brand shook his head fast and hard, the temptation so strong it nearly consumed his

127

will. Nearly all his worthy intentions had been destroyed as it was.

"Can I?" she repeated.

He squeezed his eyes closed and shook his head. For good measure, he added verbally. "No."

"You're sure?"

Hell, no, he wasn't sure of anything at this point, but his mind was beginning to interject cool reason, and he took hold of it with both hands. How easy it would be for him to set aside their problems and make love to her until she saw matters his way. Once they'd crossed the physical barriers, Brand was certain, he could convince her to marry him. If he'd been a different kind of man, he might have done it, but Brand was convinced he'd hate himself for manipulating her, and eventually so would Erin. He couldn't risk that.

Once he'd composed himself, he turned around and held out his hand to her. She slipped into his embrace, her arms cradling his middle.

"Why?"

Once again Brand didn't require an explanation. She was asking why he hadn't made love to her.

"We're not ready."

He felt her lips form a smile against the hollow of his throat. "You could have fooled me."

Brand eased her away from him, holding

her at arm's length, his hands braced against her shoulders. "We'll make love when we've reached a compromise. I'm not going to fall into the habit of settling our differences in bed, and that's exactly what would happen. I'm not looking to have an affair with you, Erin. I want a permanent relationship."

Her shoulders sagged, and her head dropped. "There isn't any compromise for us."

"There is if we want it bad enough."

Erin felt herself weakening against the powerful force of Brand's personality. If only Brand weren't so incredibly stubborn. He claimed he didn't want them to complicate their feelings for each other by hopping into bed with one another. Good grief, a woman was supposed to be the one seeking commitment. If she wanted to make love, which she obviously had, then he should "damn the torpedoes" and comply with her wishes. But oh, no, he wouldn't do that! He had to complicate everything by being decent and honorable.

If she'd had her way, they'd be in bed this very moment. She was so eager to relinquish her virginity that she'd practically thrown herself at him. Erin's cheeks grew pink as she remembered the way she'd begged him to make love to her. She'd never been so brazen with anyone in her life. Not even in her wildest fantasies with Neal.

Neal was her make-believe lover. Okay, it was silly — stupid, even — but during college, she and her best friend, Terry, had read several books about setting goals and achieving dreams. Each and every one of those self-help books had claimed that one had to learn to visualize whatever it was one wanted in life.

One Saturday afternoon, when they were bored and lonely, convinced they were destined to live their lives alone, Erin and Terry had conjured up the perfect husband. Terry had named her lover Earl, and Erin had chosen Neal, because she liked the sound of the name on her tongue.

Last summer Terry had met and married a man she claimed was exactly like the one she'd created. Erin had flown to New Mexico for the wedding.

Brand, however, had little in common with her dream lover. Both men were tall, dark and handsome, naturally. If it were the physical attributes that concerned her most, then Brand would fill the bill perfectly. In fact, he was more attractive than anything she'd ever expected in a man.

Neal, however, had roots buried so deep they reached all the way to the center of the earth. He was from a well-established pioneer family. His great-great-grandfather had battled Indians and helped settle the area — not

Seattle in particular, but *any* area.

He'd been born and raised in the same house. A home built on a corner, bordered by a tall, fenced backyard. Erin didn't know why she'd decided on the corner house with the fenced yard, but it had a nice secure feel to it.

Once they were married, she and Neal would buy a house themselves, and it, too, would be on a corner. Once children arrived, they'd fence it, as well.

Her ideal man would have been popular in school, and his senior-class president. He was well liked and trusted by all who knew him. As for his profession, Erin saw him as a banker or an attorney or something equally stable. If he was offered a huge promotion, if it meant moving, he'd never accept it. His home and his extended family were every-thing to him. He wouldn't dream of up-rooting his wife and children for something as fleeting as a career opportunity.

Neal wasn't wealthy. Money had never con-cerned Erin much, although it would be nice if he did happen to have a healthy savings account, since she tended to live paycheck-to-paycheck.

For the past several years, whenever Erin had dated someone new — which she hated to admit hadn't been that often — she'd compared him to Neal. Her ideal man. The visualization of her dream husband.

Although Brand and Neal might be relatively close in physical attributes, they were worlds apart in every other area.

"What did you just say?" Brand asked, nuzzling her ear with his nose. They were sitting on the sofa, watching an old television movie. Most of the day had been spent walking around the Seattle Center, the site of the 1962 World's Fair, and talking. Although they'd talked for hours on end, neither of them had spoken about their situation again or discussed their options.

"I said something?" Erin asked, surprised.

"Yes. It sounded like 'Tell Brand about Neal.' "

"I said that out loud?" She scooted away from him and sat on the edge of the cushion, pressing her elbows into her knees. This habit of voicing her thoughts was growing worse all the time. Nothing was sacred anymore.

"Who's Neal?"

"A . . . friend," she stammered, not daring to look at him. If she were to let Brand know that Neal was just part of her fantasy world, he'd book her into the nearest hospital and request a mental evaluation.

"A friend," Brand repeated thoughtfully. "Competition?"

"In a manner of speaking."

"Why didn't you mention him before now?" Brand's voice had tightened slightly.

It seemed the perfect opportunity to pretend Neal was real, but that would mean lying to Brand, and Erin didn't know that she could do it. She'd had such little practice at telling lies, and Brand would probably see through it in a second.

"I haven't seen Neal in a while," she answered, stalling for time. She had to think fast, milk this opportunity for all it was worth and prove to Brand that she wasn't as naive or as guileless as he seemed to believe.

"So he's a friend you haven't seen in a while?"

"That's correct. Are you jealous?"

"Insanely so. Do I need to worry about him?"

"That depends."

"On what?" he demanded.

"Several things." She stretched and, leaning back, relaxed against him, tucking her feet beneath her.

It was all the invitation Brand needed. His hands stroked the length of her arms as he buried his mouth against her hair and said, "I'm not too worried."

"Good. There's really no reason for you to be."

Brand slipped his mouth a little higher and nibbled at her earlobe. At the heated flow of tingling pleasure, she carefully edged away from him, unfolding her feet.

Brand caught her by the shoulders and

brought her back against him. He pushed his fingers through her hair, lifting it away from the side of her neck, and kissed her there, his tongue moist and hot.

"As I said before," Brand murmured against her throat. "I'm not concerned."

"Maybe you should be. He's got a steady job. Roots."

"So do I."

A tiny smile edged up her lips. "Perhaps, but your roots are shallow and easily transplanted. Maybe you should consider Neal competition."

"Is that so?" He twisted her around and pressed her back against the sofa cushion, poising himself above her. His eyes held hers, reading her as best he could. Erin didn't dare blink.

Slowly he lowered his head to the valley between her breasts and flicked his tongue over the warm flesh. His fingers laid open her lacy bra with a dexterity that should have shocked her, and in fact, did.

Erin clasped his head and sighed with welcome and relief as his mouth latched hungrily on a nipple and feasted heavily. The things he did to her breasts felt so good, so wonderful. To have him come to her like this, as if he were familiar with every part of her womanly body, as if the passion and the intimacy they shared made everything right. She arched and buckled beneath him, having trouble thinking coherently. He didn't help matters any by transferring his attention to the other breast.

Brand made everything feel right. Such thinking was bound to lead her into trouble. Erin might as well believe she could walk on water or leap off a tall building without the least bit of worry as have him make love to her like this.

As nonsensical as it was, having Brand touch her caused all the problems in the world to fade from view. All the conflict between them shriveled up and died a quick and silent death. With her breasts filling his mouth and his hands creating a magic and a heat that threatened to bring her to that earth-shattering sensual explosion, there was no room for anything but feeling. No room for doubt. No room for fear. No room for questions.

His kiss raked her mouth while his hands shaped and molded her breasts, lifting them so that the hardened, excited peaks rubbed against the rough fabric of his shirt. She longed to feel her flesh against his, and she worked toward that end, nearly tearing the material as she tugged it free from his waist. After she popped one button, Brand pushed her eager hands aside and unfastened the few remaining buttons himself. With his help, she was able to peel off the only barrier between them, thin as it was.

Brand lowered himself to her, and the sensation of her warm, heated flesh against the masculine roughness of his hard chest caused her to close her eyes and cry out in pleasure.

Brand subdued her whimper with a kiss, plunging his tongue deep in her mouth. His hips moved against hers, telegraphing his urgent need for her. Erin wanted him, too, and instinctively countered each of his movements with one of her own.

Pressing her hand between them, she stroked the hard outline of his maleness. Brand groaned against her mouth, and when he drew in a deep breath, she could feel the rumbling in his chest against the softness of her breasts. She reached for the snap of his jeans, but he pushed her fumbling hand aside and released it himself.

He kissed the side of her jaw and teased the seam of her lips with his tongue. "You're proving to be too much of a temptation."

"Me? Really?" She couldn't help sounding surprised. As far as she knew, she'd never enticed a man. Certainly not to the point of arousal Brand had reached. It made her feel beautiful when she knew she wasn't, and powerful when she'd never experienced a weakness more profound.

Slowly, as if her hand weighed a great deal more than it did, he lifted it away from him and pinned it between them, flattening her palm against his chest.

"Now," he said, drawing in a slow, even breath, "reassure me."

She frowned. "About what?"

"Neal."

Her face relaxed into a slow smile. "Neal is . . . Let me put it this way . . ." No, she decided, it was too difficult to explain. "You don't need to worry about him."

"He wants you, doesn't he?"

She lowered her lashes and shook her head. "No. I shouldn't have said anything. It was a slip of the tongue, remember? Not meant for your ears."

"I don't care. I want to know who he is."

"Trust me, you don't need to worry about him. I promise."

"Is he married to someone else?"

She was beginning to regret the whole episode, especially since she'd known from the first that she wasn't going to be able to pull it off and she'd persisted anyway. Brand deserved the truth, no matter how unflattering it was.

"Neal isn't real. I made him up a long time ago when I wrote down a list of the personality traits I wanted in a husband. I shouldn't have carried it this far — It was a poor joke."

"What?" Brand exploded. After a shocked moment, he laughed, then kissed the curve of her shoulder and lightly bit her skin.

She yelped, though he hadn't hurt her.

"That's what you deserve."

"I couldn't help it. You fell into my hands."

"That isn't the only thing we fell into. Sweet heaven, Erin, either we resolve something soon, or I'm going back to Hawaii unfit for military service."

The reminder that he would be leaving within a few hours robbed them of laughter and fun and shared passions like a thief in the night.

Slowly, reluctantly, he eased himself off her and then helped Erin into a sitting position. He continued to hold her for several minutes, his chin resting against the crown of her head.

Neither spoke. But the silence wasn't an uneasy one. Both of them seemed not to want or need to fill the void with idle chatter. Perhaps because they were afraid of what there was to say.

He was leaving, and it was something Erin had to accept. If they were to continue their relationship, it would be something he'd do countless times. Soon she'd end up keeping tabs on the times they said goodbye.

Later, Brand insisted on taking her to a plush restaurant. The food was excellent. They talked some more, but once again they avoided the subject that was uppermost in their minds.

"So how's Margo?" he asked over coffee when a sudden silence fell between them.

"Margo . . . Oh, I'd forgotten I'd told you about her. She's doing better than I expected," Erin said, and then added, "but she's having her share of problems, too. Mostly she's having a difficult time dealing with her anger. A few weeks back I recommended she attend an anger-management course."

"Has she always had trouble with that?"

"Apparently not, but we're not dealing with someone with a hot temper. What Margo is experiencing is rage. There are times when she literally wants to kill her husband for what he's done to her and their marriage. As more and more of the details of his 'other life' come into play, she's having to face head-on the deception and the pain, and that isn't easy for anyone. She feels betrayed and abandoned, in addition to being confused and lost. There was one bright spot, however. She got her driver's license recently, and I believe once she experiences the freedom a car will give her she's going to adjust a whole lot better."

Brand sipped his coffee, his eyes warm and thoughtful. "Doesn't being around these women affect you?"

"How do you mean?"

"Your attitude?"

"Toward marriage?"

Brand nodded.

"I've seen plenty of good marriages, my own mother and father's included. I —"

"Just a minute," Brand interrupted. "You mean to say your parents, who've been married how many years?"

"Thirty."

"They've been married thirty years and they're happy."

It didn't take a genius to see where Brand was leading the conversation. "You can stop right now, Brandon Davis. My mother is a special kind of woman. She thrived on adventure, and don't let anyone kid you, transporting everything you own from one port to another is an adventure, mostly the unpleasant variety."

"She liked it?"

"Liked isn't the word I'd use. Mom accepted it. When Dad announced he had shipping orders, she'd simply smile and dutifully do what had to be done, without question, without regret."

"I see. And you —"

She raised her hand. "Don't even ask." A short silence fell over them. "We're doing it again," Erin said after several tension-filled moments.

"Arguing?"

"No," she answered, her coffee capturing her attention. "We've done it almost the entire length of your stay."

"Done what?"

"Talked about everything else." After he'd first arrived, they'd discussed their relationship only briefly. It was something of a wonder how they'd masterfully avoided the subject for as long as they had. They'd talked about her Women In Transition class, her job with the King County Community Action Program and Marilyn — alias Margo — at length. Even Aimee and her troubled marriage had entered into their conversation.

Sometimes they'd spend hours on a single subject. Brand was an easy person to talk to. He listened and seemed genuinely interested in every aspect of her life, sharing her love and concern for others.

In retrospect, she understood their reluctance to discuss their own relationship, or rather their lack of one.

"There's no solution for us," she said, swamped with melancholy. They couldn't continue to fool themselves. Sooner or later they'd be forced to face the impossibility of their situation. Brand was one hundred percent Navy. As it had been with her father, it was with him. The military was far more than his career; it was his life.

"Of course, there's a solution," Brand countered.

"You could leave the navy and find work here in Seattle," she offered, but even as she spoke, Erin realized that plan wasn't feasible.

Brand would be miserable outside of the military, just as unhappy as she'd be as part of it.

He mulled over her suggestion for a time. "I wish settling in Seattle was that easy, but it isn't."

"I know," she answered bitterly. Glancing at her watch, she moved her gaze from her wrist to him. "Shouldn't we be leaving?"

Brand looked at his own watch. "We still have time."

Erin wasn't convinced of that. But she wasn't as worried about Brand making his transport plane as she was about having to tell him goodbye. This time was going to be far more difficult than the first, and the third even more heart-wrenching than the second. It would go on and on and on until they were both so much in love and so wretched they'd be willing to agree to anything just to end the heartache.

"There'll never be any easy answers for us," she whispered through the tightening knot of truth. "One of us will end up giving in to the other and spending the rest of our lives wishing we hadn't."

"You're right," Brand announced abruptly. "Now that you mention it, I believe it is time we left." He stood and slapped his linen napkin on the table.

Erin noted how tense the muscles of his jaw had become. Silently she did as he asked, excusing herself while he paid the tab.

Once she was inside the powder room, Erin leaned against the sink, needing its support. If she didn't compose herself, she was going to break down and weep right there.

She had to put an end to this torment for both their sakes. Brand didn't seem to want to listen to reason. From everything he'd said, he seemed to believe a magical, mystical fairy godmother would swoop down out of the heavens and declare the perfect solution and they'd all live happily ever after. It simply wasn't going to happen.

By the time she reappeared, Brand was standing outside waiting for her. The night was cool, the stars obliterated by a thick overcast and the threat of rain hung heavy in the air.

Brand greeted her with "I think it would be best if we said goodbye here."

Her heart objected loud and strong, but she didn't voice a single doubt. "You're probably right."

"Well," he said after expelling his breath. "This is it."

"Right," she returned. "Have a safe trip."

"I will."

How stiff and unemotional he sounded, as if they were little more than acquaintances.

"Are you sure you don't want me to go to the airport with —"

"No."

She nodded, feeling wretched. This was worse than she'd ever believed it would be. Her throat had closed off, and she couldn't have carried on a conversation had her life depended on it. One- or two-word replies were all she could manage.

"Yes," he countered, just as quickly. "Come with me. God help us both, Erin. I can't bear to say goodbye to you like this."

Chapter Seven

The phone was ringing when Erin walked in the door that evening. She rushed into the kitchen to answer it, her heart racing like a steam engine. She frantically prayed it was Brand and that he wouldn't give up before she could make it to the phone. All the while she was dashing across the house she cursed herself, because she was famished for the sound of his voice, eager to accept each little crumb he tossed her way, despite all her vows to the contrary.

She'd gone to the airport with him, kissed him goodbye, then stood and waited until his plane had taxied down the runway and shot into the sky, taking him away from her. Like a fool, she'd stood there for what seemed like an eternity, her heart aching, while she chided herself for caring so damn much. Now she was doing it all again. Running through her own home, risking life and limb in an effort to reach the phone, praying it was Brand who was trying to contact her.

"Hello," she answered breathlessly, nearly tearing the phone off the wall in her eagerness to get to it in time. While her breathing returned to normal, she was forced to listen to a twenty-second campaign from a professional carpet-cleaning company.

By the time she replaced the receiver, Erin was shaking with irritation. Not because she was angry with the salesperson, but simply because the caller hadn't been Brand.

He'd left two weeks earlier, and she'd heard from him twice by phone. A handful of letters had arrived, and although she treasured each one, she found something important was lacking in this second batch. Something Erin couldn't quite put her finger on. Each letter was filled with details of his life, but she felt Brand was holding back a part of himself from her, protecting his heart in much the same way she was shielding hers.

She'd written him a number of times herself, but she'd always been careful about what she told him. Anyone reading her letters would assume she and Brand were nothing more than good friends.

After he'd left the second time, she'd battled with the right and wrong of continuing a long-distance relationship. Over the years she'd repeatedly promised herself she wouldn't allow this very thing to happen, yet here she was involved with a navy man! Her principles had vanished like topsoil in a flash flood. Past experience had taught her that Brand wouldn't give up on her, and frankly, she hadn't the strength to sever things on her own.

Her plan was to subtly phase herself out of

his life. But the strategy had backfired on her. Each day she found herself hungering for word from him, convinced this separation was far more difficult than the one before.

Erin dreamed of Brand that night. He'd come to her when she was in bed, warm and cozy, missing him dreadfully. Slipping under the covers, he'd reached for her, his eyes wide with unspoken need. His kisses were hot and hungry as he buried his mouth in hers.

In the beginning, Erin had tried to hold back, not wanting the kisses to deepen for fear of where they would lead. Gradually, without Brand ever saying a word, she felt herself opening to him. She was lost in the wonder of his arms, and he seemed to be equally absorbed in hers. Both seemed on the brink of being found, of discovering heaven.

His body had moved over hers, his skin hot to the touch and as smooth as velvet. The clothes that had been a protective barrier between them seemed to melt away. Bare, heated skin had met bare, heated skin, and they'd both sighed at the mysterious joy found in such simple pleasure.

His hands caressed her, his touch light and unbelievably gentle. His kisses robbed her of her sanity, and when he moved above her, she parted her thighs and moaned in welcome.

"Do you like this?" he whispered close to her ear.

"Oh . . . yes," she assured him.

His hands cupped her buttocks while his kiss raked her mouth. By the time he finished, Erin was panting and weak with longing. "Make love to me," she pleaded. "Brand, please, don't make me wait . . . not again."

In response, he lowered his sleek, muscular body to hers. Thrilled and excited, Erin opened to him, wanting him so badly she clawed at his back, needing him to hurry and give her what she craved.

To her dismay, he didn't enter her. She squirmed and closed her legs around the hot staff of his manhood, arching and buckling as he began to move, sliding between her thighs, the friction moistened by her excitement and need.

"Brand," she pleaded again, her voice hoarse as she clutched at him, breathing hard and fast. "Give me what I want."

"No . . ." His voice was that of a man in torment.

"Yes." She thought to outwit him, and she rotated her hips so that his thrust met the apex of her womanhood. If he were to continue, penetration couldn't be avoided, and he would fill her the way she craved. Arching her neck, she lifted her hips, coaxing him to completion, wanting him so much she couldn't think clearly.

"Please," she begged, tilting her hips higher and higher, but he stopped short. "I want to feel all of you. . . . Oh, Brand . . ."

"No . . . no . . ." He sounded like a man pounding against the gates of heaven, lost for all eternity. "We can't . . . It isn't right, not now, not yet. Soon," he promised. "Soon."

"We can . . . we must."

Her cries and pleas seemed to have no effect on him, and try as she might with her body, pushing her hips forward, inviting him, even demanding that he give her what she sought, did no good.

He was full and hard, and he teased her until a violent release delivered her physically from the prison of unfulfilled desire. She lay panting, her eyes closed, physically relieved but emotionally starving.

It was then that Erin had woken.

For a long while, she stared up at the ceiling, her head spinning, her heart pounding. She'd never been one to put a lot of stock in dreams, but this one had been so vivid, so real, that she couldn't help being affected.

This was the way it would be with Brand. It wasn't that he'd cruelly refuse to make love to her, but he'd never be able to satisfy the deep inner longings of her soul.

She required more than he could ever supply.

And they both knew it.

Each day that followed, Erin reassured herself nothing good would be accomplished by loving Brand. She'd made a decent life for herself, and she wasn't going to leave the only security she'd ever found because a few hormones refused to let her forget she was a woman.

She repeated the same tired arguments to herself in the mirror every morning and then went about her day. But when the nights arrived, her dreams were filled with loving Brand. Not all her dreams were wild sexual romps. When they did come, she found herself left frustrated and miserable. More often, her nights would be full of memories of him and the scant time they had spent together. Brand and she would be walking, hand in hand, along the beach together, talking, laughing, appreciating the love they'd discovered in each other. Then Brand would take her in his arms and kiss her until her mouth was moist and swollen. His eyes would delve into hers while his hands tenderly brushed the red curls from the side of her face.

They'd kiss, and their lips would cling, then kiss again, slowly, lazily, savoring each other.

Each morning, when Erin woke, it was the ending.

Each night, when she climbed beneath the sheets, was the beginning.

Stunned, Brand sat at his desk, reading over the same words two and three times. He felt numb. He'd been assigned duty aboard the command ship USS *Blue Ridge*. The *Blue Ridge* was the flagship of the Seventh Fleet and was being deployed in the western Pacific. Tour of duty — six months.

This couldn't have come at a worse time for him. Without a doubt, he knew he was going to lose Erin.

There wasn't a damn thing he could do about it.

A feeling of helplessness and frustration engulfed him like a tidal wave.

He'd left Seattle with matters unsettled, but that couldn't be avoided. He'd continued to write her every day since, and all he'd gotten in return were chatty letters that didn't say a damn thing about what she was feeling or thinking. He might as well be corresponding with a troop of Girl Scouts. Reading Erin's letters was like reading the newspaper. Just the facts, listed as unemotionally as possible. She even signed off with "Best Wishes." Well, Brand had a few wishes of his own, but Erin didn't seem to be interested in fulfilling any of those.

"Six months," he said aloud. It might as well be an eternity. Erin would refuse to wait for him; she'd made that clear from the first. She'd start dating other men, and the thought produced an ache that cut through his heart and his pride.

Although Brand had made light of it when she'd brought up this Neal character, he'd been jealous as hell. When he'd learned Neal was a figment of her imagination, the relief he'd felt was overwhelming.

Erin was a rare jewel, undiscovered and unappreciated by those around her. At first glance, few would have declared her beautiful. Her hair was a little too red, her nose a bit too sharp, her mouth a tad too full, for her beauty to be considered classic. But upon closer examination, she was a precious pearl, worth selling everything he owned to possess.

Brand understood from the things she'd told him how seldom she dated. She was endearingly shy. Warm, gracious, caring.

And Brand loved her.

He loved her so much he hadn't been able to function properly since he'd returned from his evaluation assignment at Sand Point.

He had to tell her about being assigned sea duty, of course, and he tried doing so in a letter several times. After attempting to phrase it a number of ways, jokingly, seriously, thoughtfully and playfully, Brand resigned himself to contacting her by phone.

He delayed it, probably longer than he should have.

He announced it flat out, without pre-amble.

And waited.

"Well," he said, speaking into the receiver. "Say something."

"Bon voyage."

"Come on, Erin, I'm serious."

"So am I."

She had this flippant way about her when she was upset and trying not to show it. Brand had anticipated it and allowed for her sarcasm, but she was precariously close to angering him.

"You want me to act surprised?" Erin questioned. "I can't find it in me. We both knew sooner or later that you'd get your shipping orders. You are in the navy. You should expect sea duty."

"I want you to wait for me." There, he'd said it. He hadn't softened it with romantic words or sent the message attached to a dozen red roses. Just the plain truth. These were going to be the longest months of his life, simply because he'd never left a woman he loved behind until now. He didn't like the feeling. Not one damn bit.

Erin didn't respond.

"Did you hear me?" he asked her, raising his voice. "I want you to wait for me."

"No." She said it so matter-of-factly, as if the answer took little, if any, thought or con-sideration.

That pricked Brand's pride, but he should have been used to it by now with Erin. Offhand he could have named two or three women who would have broken into tears when they learned he'd been assigned sea duty. In a few cases, the women had promised undying faithfulness and loyalty. They'd stood on the pier weeping as he'd pulled out of port, and they'd been there happy and excited upon his return. Brand hadn't expected the same reaction from Erin — in fact, hysterical women were a turnoff as far as he was concerned — but he needed something more than what Erin was offering him.

"So in other words you plan to date someone else?" he demanded.

"Yes."

"Who?"

"That's none of your business."

"The hell it isn't." His voice was raised and angry. "I'm in love with you, Erin MacNamera, and —"

"I didn't ask you to love me. I'm not even sure I want you to love me. Go ahead, go off and play navy for the next six months, but I'm telling you right now, Brand Davis, I won't sit home twiddling my thumbs waiting for you."

When Erin replaced the telephone receiver, there were tears glistening in her eyes. She hated being weak, hated the emotion that clogged her throat and knotted her fists at her side.

So Brand would be spending the next six months sailing between Hong Kong, the Philippines and several other exotic ports. Great. She was pleased for him. Happy, even.

It was the end for them. It was over. Done. Finished.

At first, when she'd answered the phone, the excitement she felt hearing Brand's voice had taken the sting from his words. He must have known how she would react to his news and been worried about telling her, because he'd barely answered her greeting before launching into the dreary details of this six-month assignment. To be fair, he hadn't sounded any too pleased about going out to sea himself, but that didn't change anything.

He'd leave without a qualm and without question. Why? Because the navy owned him the way it did her father and everyone else she'd grown up with, and she hated it.

But the United States Navy would never own her again. Never!

Brand had paused after telling her — waiting, it seemed, for some response from her. Her reaction had been immediate, but she'd shared damn little of it with Brand. When reality had begun to sink in, a deep sense of anger, loss, resentment and fear had crowded in around her like teenagers against the stage at a rock concert.

It was the same indescribable sensation that had come over her every time her father had announced he'd received a new assignment and they'd be moving.

Those identical emotions stormed at her once again. She felt like a casualty of a major disaster. Homeless. Lost emotionally and physically. Wandering around in the blue haze of insecurities that came when everything familiar, everything comfortable, had been pulled out from under her feet.

Erin had thought to escape that feeling for the rest of her life. She couldn't, wouldn't, allow Brand to drag her back into that crazy lifestyle.

"I'm going to miss loving you," she spoke into the stillness of the room.

She *would* miss Brand. As silly as it seemed, she'd miss the loneliness of waiting for his calls. The joy of his coming and the pain of his leaving. All those were part of the man she had to learn to stop loving.

The following morning, Erin called in sick. Unfortunately, it was Aimee who answered the phone.

"You don't sound sick," her friend announced first thing. "In fact, you sound as if you've sat up all night crying. I can hear it in your voice."

"I . . . Just write me down as sick, would

you? Tell Eve I've got the flu, or make up some other excuse." She finished by hic-cuping on a sob.

"Aha! So I was right, you have been crying. What's wrong, sweetie?"

"Nothing."

"You think you're fooling me? Think again, girl!"

"Come on, Aimee," Erin mumbled. "Be nice. I don't want to talk about it."

"It must be Brand. What did he do that was so terrible this time? Send you roses? Tell you you're beautiful?"

"He's going out to sea for six months," she blurted out, as though someone should arrest him for even considering leaving her feeling the way she did. "He hasn't had sea duty in two years. He met me, and wham — the navy puts the kiss of death on anything developing between us. I . . . couldn't be more pleased. . . . It couldn't have come at a better time."

"You don't mean a word of that. Listen, I've got a light schedule this morning. How about if I drop in and we have one of our heart-to-heart talks. It sounds like you could use one."

"All right," Erin agreed, "only . . . hurry, would you?"

Aimee arrived around ten. Erin was dressed in her housecoat and her fuzzy pink slippers with the open toes. Her mother had sent her the shoes the Christmas before last, and just then Erin needed something from home.

She carried the tissue box with her to the door, blew her nose and then carelessly tossed the used Kleenex on the carpet.

Aimee walked into the house and followed the trail of discarded tissues into the kitchen. "Good grief, it looks like you held a wake in here."

"The funny part is," Erin said, sobbing and laughing both at the same time, "I don't even know why I'm crying. So Brand's going off to sea. Big deal. It isn't like I didn't anticipate he would. He's navy."

"You're in love with him is why." Standing on tiptoe, Aimee reached inside Erin's tallest cupboard and brought down a teapot. "Sit down," she said, pointing toward the table. "I'll brew us some tea."

"There's coffee made."

"You need tea."

Erin wasn't sure she understood, but she wasn't in any mood to question her friend's illogical wisdom. If Aimee wanted to brew her a strong cup of tea, then far be it from her to argue.

"I've learned something important," Erin announced once Aimee had joined her.

"Oh?" Her co-worker reached across the table for the sugar bowl and added a liberal amount to Erin's cup. "Tell me."

"I've decided falling in love is the most wonderful, most . . . creative, most incredible feeling in the world."

"Yes," Aimee agreed with some reluctance. "It can be."

"But at the same time it's the most destructive, painful, distressing emotion I've ever experienced."

"Welcome to the real world. If it were only the first part, we'd all make a point of falling in love regularly. Unfortunately, it involves a whole lot more."

"I always thought it was roses and sunshine and sharing a glass of expensive wine while sitting in front of a brick fireplace. I had no idea it was so . . . so painful."

"It can be." Aimee held the delicate china cup with both hands. "Trust me, I know exactly what you're going through."

"You do?"

Her friend nodded. "Steve moved out of the house last weekend. We've decided to contact our respective lawyers. It's going to be a challenge to see which one of us can file for the divorce first."

Erin couldn't hold back her gasp of surprise. "You didn't say anything earlier in the week."

"What's there to say? It isn't something I want to announce to the office, not that you'd spread the word. The way I figure it, everyone's going to find out sooner or later anyway, and personally, I prefer later."

"How are you feeling?"

Aimee gave an inelegant shrug. "All right, I guess. It isn't like this mess happened overnight. Steve and I haven't been getting along for the last couple of years. Frankly, it's something of a relief that he's gone."

Erin could understand what her friend was saying. The break with Brand had been inevitable. She'd delayed it too long as it was, hoping they'd come up with a solution, a means of compromise, anything that would make what they shared work.

"What we need is a plan of action," Aimee announced with characteristic enthusiasm. "Something that's going to get us both through this with our minds intact."

"Shopping?" Erin suggested.

"You're joking? I can't afford panty hose until payday, and on the advice of my attorney I dare not use the credit cards."

"What, then?" Everything Erin could think of involved money.

Gnawing at the corner of her mouth, Aimee mulled over their dilemma. "I think we should start dating again."

"Dating?" Erin sounded doubtful. "But you're still married, and I'm not interested right now . . . Maybe later."

"You're right. Dating is a bit drastic. It sounds simple enough, but where the hell would we find men? The bowling alley?"

160

"But I don't think we should rule out casual relationships," Erin qualified. "Nothing serious, of course."

"Next month, then. We'll give ourselves a few weeks to mentally prepare for reentering the dating scene. We'll diet and change our hair and get beautiful all over again and wow 'em."

In a month Erin might consider the idea, but for now it left her cold. "What about now? How are we going to get through . . . today?"

"Well . . ." Aimee paused. "I think we're both going to have to learn to survive," she said, and her small voice quavered.

Erin handed her a fresh tissue. They hugged each other, promising to support one another.

"Love is hell," Erin blubbered.

"So is being alone," Aimee whispered.

Brand stood in front of the telephone and stared at the numbers for a long while. He'd had a couple of drinks, and although his mind was crystal-clear, he wasn't sure contacting Erin was the thing to do, especially now.

Damn it all, the woman had him tied up in knots a sailor couldn't undo. He was due to ship out in a few days, but if he didn't clear up this matter with Erin, it would hang over his head for the entire six months. He couldn't go to sea with matters unsettled between them the way they were.

More than likely she'd slam the phone down in his ear.

What the hell? It was either phone her or regret the fact he hadn't. Brand had learned early in his career that it wasn't the things he'd done that he regretted, it was the things he *hadn't* done.

"What's the worst that can happen?" he asked himself aloud, amused that he'd picked up Erin's habit of talking to herself.

He answered himself. "She can say no."

"She's as good as turned you down before," his other self argued.

"Quit talking and just do it."

Following his own advice, Brand punched out the numbers that would connect him with his beautiful Irish rose. The phone rang seven times before she answered.

"Hello." She sounded groggy, as if he'd gotten her out of bed. The picture of her standing there in her kitchen, her hair mussed and her body warm and supple, was enough to tighten his loins.

"Erin? It's Brand."

"Brand?" She elevated her voice with what Brand felt certain must be happiness. She loved him. She might try to convince herself otherwise, but she was crazy about him.

"Hello, darling."

"Do you have any idea what time it is?" she demanded.

"Nope. Is it late?"

"You've been drinking."

Now that sounded like an accusation, one he didn't take kindly to. "I've had a couple of drinks. I was celebrating."

"Why'd you call me? You sound three sheets to the wind, Lieutenant."

Brand closed his eyes and leaned his shoulder against the wall. If he tried hard enough, he might be able to pretend Erin was in the same room with him. He needed her. He loved her, and, damn it all, he wanted her with him, especially when he wasn't going to be able to hold or kiss her for six long months.

"Brand," she repeated. "I'm standing here in my stocking feet, shivering. I'd bet cold cash you didn't phone because you were looking for a way to waste your hard-earned money, now did you?"

"I love you, darling."

His words were met with silence.

"Come on, Erin, don't be so cruel. Tell me what you feel. I need to hear it."

"I think we should both go back to bed and forget we ever had this conversation."

Brand groaned. "Come on, sweetheart. I never realized how stingy you are with your affections."

"Brand . . ."

"All right, all right, if you insist, I'll tell you why I phoned. Only — Hold on a minute, will you?" He set the phone down on the table, then climbed down on one knee. It took some doing, because the floor insisted upon buckling under his feet. He didn't drink often, and a few shots of good Irish whiskey had affected him far more than he'd realized.

"Brand, what the hell are you doing?"

"I'm ready now," he whispered. Drawing in a deep breath, he started speaking once more. "Can you hear me?"

"Of course I can hear you."

"Good." Now that it had come time, Brand discovered he was shaking like a leaf caught in a whirlwind. His heart was pounding like an automatic hammer. "Erin MacNamera, I love you, and I'm asking you on bended knee to become my wife."

Chapter Eight

Standing on the bridge, a pair of binoculars clenched tightly in his hands, Brand stared at mile upon mile of open sea. The horizon was marked by an endless expanse of blue, cloudless sky. The wind was brisk, carrying with it the scent of salt and sea. Taking in deep breaths, Brand dragged several lungfuls of the fresh air through his chest.

This was his second week sailing the waters of the Pacific. Generally Brand relished sea duty. There was a special part of his soul that found solace while at sea. He felt removed from the frantic activity of life on the land, set apart in a time and place for reconciliation with himself and his world.

Brand was grateful for sea duty, especially now, with the way matters had worked out with Erin. These next few months would give him the necessary time to heal.

Erin was out of his life. But he still loved her. He probably always would feel something very special for her. He'd analyzed his feelings a thousand times, hoping to gain perspective. He'd discovered that the depth, the strength, of his love wasn't logical or even reasonable. She'd made her views plain from the day they met, yet he'd egotistically disregarded everything she'd claimed and fallen for her anyway. Now he had to work like hell to get her out of his mind.

She'd flatly turned down his proposal of marriage. At first, after he'd asked her on bended knee, she'd tried to make light of it, claiming it was the liquor talking. Brand had assured her otherwise. He loved her enough to want to spend the rest of his life with her. He wanted her to be the mother of his children and to grow old with him. She'd gotten serious then and started to weep softly. At least Brand chose to believe those were tears, although Erin had tried hard to make him believe she was actually laughing at the implausibility of them ever finding happiness together.

She claimed his proposal was a last-ditch effort on his part, and on that account Erin might have been right. The fear of losing her had consumed him from the moment he'd received his orders. Rightly so, as it had worked out.

So Erin was out of his life. He'd given it his best shot, been willing to do almost anything to keep her, but it hadn't worked. In retrospect, he could be pragmatic about their relationship. It was time to move on. Heal. Grow. Internalize what he'd learned from loving her.

One thing was sure. Brand wasn't going to

fall in love again any time soon. It hurt too damn much.

The breeze picked up, and the wind whipped around his face. He squinted into the sun, more determined than ever to set Erin from his mind.

Erin's philosophy in life was relatively simple. Take one day at a time and treat others as she expected to be treated herself. The part about not dating anyone in the military and not overcharging her credit cards was an uncomplicated down-to-earth approach to knowing herself.

Then why had she bought a grand piano?

Erin had asked herself that question ten times over the past several days. She'd been innocently walking through the mall one Saturday afternoon, browsing. She certainly hadn't intended to make a major purchase. Innocently she'd happened into a music store, looking for a cassette tape by one of her favorite artists, and paused in front of the polished mahogany piano.

There must have been something about her that caught the salesman's attention, because he'd sauntered over and casually asked her if she played.

Erin didn't, but she'd always wanted to learn. From that point until the moment the piano was scheduled to be delivered to the house, Erin had repeatedly asked herself what

167

she was doing purchasing an ultraexpensive grand piano.

"How many credit cards did it take?" Aimee had asked her, aghast, when she heard what Erin had done.

"Three. I'd purposely kept the amount I could borrow low on all my cards. I never dreamed I'd spend that much money at one time."

Running her hand over the keyboard, Aimee slowly shook her head. "It's a beautiful piece of furniture."

"The salesman gave me the name of a lady who teaches piano lessons, and before you know it I'll be another Van Cliburn." Erin forced a note of enthusiasm into her voice, but it fell short of any real excitement.

"That sounds great." Aimee's own level of zeal was decidedly low.

In retrospect, Erin understood why she'd done something so crazy as to buy an expensive musical instrument on her credit cards. The two men who'd delivered the piano had explained it to her without even knowing her psychological makeup.

"I hope you don't intend to move for a long time, lady," the short, round-faced man had said once they'd maneuvered the piano up her front steps.

Getting the piano into the house had been even more of a problem. Her living room was compact as it was, and the deliverymen had been forced to remove the desk and rearrange the furniture before they found space enough for the overly large piano.

"If you do decide to move, I'd include the piano in the sale of the house," the second man had said to her as he used his kerchief to wipe the sweat from his brow. His face had been red, and his face had glistened with perspiration.

"I don't plan on moving," she'd been quick to assure them both.

"It's a damn good thing," the first had muttered on his way out the door.

"If you do plan on moving out of the area, don't call us," the second had joked.

Brand had been gone one month, and Erin had maxed out three credit cards with the purchase of one grand piano. It didn't matter that she couldn't have located middle C on the keyboard to save her soul. Nor did it concern her that she'd be making payments for three years at interest rates that made the local banks giddy with glee. What did matter, Erin discovered, was that she was making a statement to herself and to Brand.

She had no intention of ever leaving Seattle. And she certainly wasn't going to allow a little thing like the United States Navy stand in the way of finding happiness. Not if it meant leaving the only roots she'd ever planted!

If Erin was actually in love with Brand —

and that *if* was as tall as the Empire State Building — then she was going to force herself to fall out of love with him.

The piano was symbolic of that. Her first move had been to reject his marriage proposal. Her second had been to purchase the piano.

Friday night Erin and Aimee met at a Mexican restaurant and ordered nachos. They'd decided earlier in the day to make an effort to have fun, drown their sorrows in good Mexican beer, and if they happened to stumble across a couple of decent-looking men, then it wouldn't hurt anyone if they were to flirt a little. For fun, Aimee had promised to give Erin lessons in attracting the opposite sex.

"We can have a good time without Steve and Brand," she insisted.

"You're absolutely right," Erin agreed. But the two of them had looked and acted so forlorn that they'd had trouble attracting a waiter's attention, let alone any good-looking, eligible men.

"You know what our problem is?" Aimee asked before stuffing a nacho in her mouth.

Erin couldn't help being flippant. "Too many jalapeños and not enough cheese?"

Aimee was quick to reply. "No. We're not trying hard enough. Then again, maybe we're trying too hard. I'm out of touch . . . I don't know what we're doing wrong."

For her part, if Erin tried any harder, the bank was going to confiscate her credit cards. As it was, she was in debt up to her eyebrows for a piano she couldn't play.

"We're trying," Erin insisted. She scanned the restaurant and frowned. It seemed every man there was sitting with a woman. Aimee was the one who claimed this place was great for meeting men, but then, her friend had been out of the singles' world for over a decade. Apparently everyone who'd met there had married and returned as couples.

"Oh, my —" Aimee gave a small cry and scooted down so far in the crescent-shaped booth that she nearly slid under the table.

"What is it?"

"Steve's here."

"Where?" Erin demanded, frantically looking around. She didn't see him in any of the booths.

"He just walked in, and . . . he's with a woman."

Erin had never met Aimee's husband, but she'd seen several pictures of him. She picked him out immediately. He was standing against the white stucco wall with a tall, thin blonde at his side. Tall and thin. Every woman's nightmare.

"You can't stay under the table the rest of the night," Erin insisted in a low whisper.

"Why should you? You don't have anything to hide."

A tense moment passed before Aimee righted herself. "You're absolutely right. I'm not the one out with a floozy." Riffling her fingers through her hair, Aimee squared her shoulders and nonchalantly reached for a nacho. She did a good job of masquerading her pain, but it was apparent, at least to Erin, that her friend was far more ruffled than she let on.

As luck would have it, Steve and his blonde strolled directly past their booth. Aimee stared straight ahead, refusing to acknowledge her husband. Erin, however, glared at him with eyes hot enough to form glass figurines.

Steve, tall and muscular, glanced over his shoulder and nearly faltered when he saw Aimee. His gaze quickly moved to Erin, and although she could have been imagining it, Erin thought he looked relieved to discover that his wife wasn't with a man.

His mouth opened, and he hesitated, apparently at a loss for words. After whispering something to his companion, he returned to Aimee and Erin's table.

"Hello, Aimee."

"Hello," she answered calmly, smiling serenely in his direction. Erin nearly did a double take. Her co-worker had been hiding under the table only a few seconds earlier.

172

"I . . . You look well."

"So do you. You remember me mentioning Erin MacNamera, don't you?"

"Of course." Steve briefly nodded in Erin's direction, but it was clear he was far more interested in talking to his wife than in exchanging pleasantries with Erin. "I . . . thought I should explain about Danielle," he said, rushing the words. "This isn't actually a date, and —"

"Steve, please, you don't owe me an explanation. Remember, you're divorcing me. It doesn't matter if you're seeing someone else. Truly it doesn't."

"I thought you were the one divorcing me."

"Are we going to squabble over every single detail? It seems a bit ridiculous, don't you think? But technically I suppose you're right. I am the one filing, so that does mean I am the one divorcing you."

"I don't want you to have the wrong impression about me and Danielle. We —"

"Don't worry about it. I'm dating again myself."

"You are?" Steve asked the question before Erin could. He straightened and frowned before continuing. "I didn't know . . . I'm sorry to have troubled you."

"It was no trouble." Once more she leveled a serene smile at him, and then she intentionally looked away, casually dismissing him.

Steve returned to the blond bombshell, and Erin stared curiously at Aimee.

"You're dating yourself?" Erin muttered under her breath. "I never expected you'd lie."

"I fully intend to date again," Aimee countered sharply. "Someday. I'm just not ready for it yet, but I will be soon enough and —" Her voice faltered, and she bit mercilessly into her lower lip. "Actually, I've lost my appetite. Would you mind terribly if we called it an evening?"

"Of course I don't mind," Erin said, glaring heatedly at Steve, who was sitting several booths down from them. But when it came right down to it, Erin didn't know who she was angriest with — Aimee, for pretending Steve didn't have the power to hurt her any longer, or Steve, who appeared equally afraid to let his wife know how much he cared. As a casual observer, Erin had to resist the urge to slap the pair of them.

The dreams returned that night. The ones where Brand climbed into bed with Erin, slipping his arms around her and nestling close to her side. There was little that was sexual about these romantic encounters, although he kissed her several times and promised to make love to her soon.

Erin woke with tears in her eyes. She didn't understand how a man who was several thousand miles away could make her feel so cherished and appreciated. Especially when she'd let it be known she didn't want anything more to do with him.

It got so that Erin welcomed the nights, praying as she drifted off to sleep that Brand would come to her as he often did.

Reality returned each morning, but it didn't seem to matter, because there were always the nights, and they were filled with such wonderful fantasies.

The letter from her father arrived a couple of weeks later.

"I received word from Brand," her father wrote in his sharply slanted scrawl. "He claims there's nothing between the two of you any longer and that's the way you want it. He was frank enough to admit he loves you, but must abide by your wishes. I couldn't believe my own eyes. Brand Davis is more man than you're likely to find in five lifetimes, and you refused his proposal? I feel I'm the one to blame for all this. I should have kept my nose out of your business. Your mother would have my hide if she knew I'd asked Brand to check up on you when he was in Seattle. To be honest, I was hoping the two of you would hit it off. If I were to handpick a husband for you, Erin, I couldn't find a better man than Brand Davis. All right, I'm a meddling old man. Your mother's right, who you date isn't any of my damn business.

"You're my daughter, Erin," he continued, "and I'll love you no matter what you decide to do in this life, but I'm telling you right now, lass, I'm downright disappointed in you."

"I've disappointed you before, Dad, and I'm likely to do so again," Erin said aloud when she'd finished the letter.

Tears smarted her eyes, but she managed to blink them back. Her father rarely spoke harshly to her, but it was apparent he'd thought long and hard about writing her this letter. It wasn't what he'd said, Erin realized, but what he'd left unsaid, that cut so deep.

Feeling restless and melancholy, Erin went for a drive that afternoon. Before she knew it, she was halfway to Oregon. Taking a side route, she drove on a twisting, narrow road that led down the Washington coast.

For a long time she sat on the beach, facing the roaring sea. The breeze whipped her hair around her face and chilled her to the bone, yet she stayed, conscious every second that somewhere out in the vast stretch of water sailed Brand, the man she was dangerously close to loving. She could pretend otherwise, buy out every store in Seattle and act as foolish as Aimee and her husband, and it wouldn't alter the fact that she loved Brand Davis.

Wrapping her arms around her bent legs, Erin rested her chin on her knees and mulled over her thoughts. The waves clamored and roared, putting up a fuss, before relinquishing and gently caressing the smooth, sandy shore. Again and again, in abject protest, the waves raged with fury and temper before ebbing. Then, tranquilly, like velvet-gloved fingers, the waves stroked the beach, leaving only a thin line of foam as a memory.

For hours, Erin sat watching the sea. In the end, before she headed back to Seattle, she hadn't reached any conclusions. She was beginning to doubt her doubts and suffer second thoughts about her second thoughts. Why, oh, why did life have to be so complicated? And why did she find the grand piano an eyesore when she walked in her front door?

Brand found order in life at sea. Internally his world felt chaotic as he struggled with his feelings for Erin. Each day that passed he grew stronger, more confident in himself.

Gradually the routine of military life gave him a strong sense of order, something to hold on to while time progressed.

Admittedly, the first weeks were rough. He found himself short-tempered, impatient and generally bad company. He worked hard and fell into his bunk at night, too tired to dream. When he did, his nights were full of Erin.

Erin at the zoo. Erin standing in the

doorway of her kitchen dressed in a sexless flannel nightgown. Erin with eyes dark enough to trap a man's soul.

He had to forget her, get her out of his system, get on with his life.

"You still hung up on MacNamera's daughter?" Brand's friend Alex Romano demanded a couple of days before they were due to dock in Hong Kong.

"Not in the least," Brand snapped, instantly regretting his short-fused temper. He smiled an apology. "Maybe I am," he admitted with some reluctance.

Alex answered with a short laugh. "I never thought I'd see the great Brand Davis go soft over a woman. It warms my heart, if you want to know the truth."

"Why's that?" Brand wasn't in the mood to play word games with his friend, but talking about Erin, even with someone who'd never met her, seemed to help. She'd dominated his thoughts for so long, he was beginning to question his own sanity.

"For one thing, it points out the fact you're human like the rest of us. We've all had women problems one time or another. But never you. At least until now. Generally women fight between themselves to fall at your feet. Personally, I never could understand it, but then I'm not much of a ladies' man."

"Ginger will be glad to hear that." Alex

and Ginger had been married for ten years and had three toddlers. Brand was godfather to the oldest boy. Although Brand was sure Alex didn't know it, in a lot of ways he was envious of his friend, of the happiness he'd found with Ginger, of the fact that there was someone waiting for him at the end of his sea duty. There was a lot to covet.

"So?" Alex pressed. "What you gonna do about MacNamera's daughter?"

Brand expelled his breath in a slow, drawn-out exercise. He'd asked Erin to marry him, offered her his heart on a silver platter, and she'd turned him down. She hadn't even needed time to think about it.

"Not a damn thing," he answered flippantly.

"Oh, dear," Alex said, and chuckled, apparently amused. "It's worse than I thought."

Maybe it was, only Brand was too stupid to admit it.

Hong Kong didn't help. During three days of shore leave, all he could do was think of Erin. He sat in a bar, nursing a glass of good Irish whisky and thinking he should take up drinking something else, because Erin was Irish. Damn little good that would do. Everything reminded Brand of Erin. He walked through the crowded streets, and when a merchant proudly brought out a piece of silk, the only thing he could picture was Erin wearing a suit made in that precise color.

The sooner they returned to sea, the better it would be.

He was wrong.

They'd sailed out of Hong Kong when her letter arrived. Brand held it in his hand for a long moment before tucking it in his shirt pocket to read later. He felt almost lightheaded by the time he made it to his cabin, where a little privacy was afforded him.

Sitting at the end of his berth, he reached for the envelope and carefully tore open the end before slipping the single sheet from inside.

Dear Brand:

I pray I'm doing the right thing by writing you. You've been gone several weeks now, and I thought, I hoped, I'd stop thinking about you.

What's troubling me most is the way our last conversation went. I'm feeling terribly guilty about the way I behaved. I was heartless and unnecessarily cruel when I didn't mean to be. Your proposal came as a shock. My only excuse is that it caught me unaware, and I didn't know what to say or how to act and so I pretended it was all a big joke. I've regretted that countless times and can only ask your forgiveness.

I bought a grand piano. I've never had lessons and can barely play a single note.

Everyone who knows me tells me I'm crazy. It wasn't until after it was delivered that I realized why I'd done anything so foolish. It was an expensive but valuable lesson. I'm taking classes now on Saturday mornings. Me and about five preteens. I strongly suspect I'm older than my teacher, but frankly I haven't gotten up enough gumption to ask. I don't know if my ego could handle that.

The others seem to find me something of a weirdo. None of them would be there if their parents weren't forcing them to take lessons. I, on the other hand, want to learn badly enough to actually pay to do so. The kids don't understand that. In four months, when you return, I should be well into book 2, and I hope to impress the hell out of you with my rendition of "Country Garden" or something swanky from Mozart. At the rate I'm progressing, I might end up playing in a cocktail lounge by age forty. Can't you just see me pounding out "Feelings" to a group of men attending an American Legion convention?

Oh, before I forget, you'll be pleased to know Margo is coming along nicely. She has her own apartment now and found a full-time job selling drapes at the J.C. Penney store. The difference in her from the first time she walked into the class until now is dramatic. She's still struggling with the pain and an occasional bout of anger, but for the most part she's doing so well. We're all proud of her. I thought you might like to hear how she's doing.

Although I've written far more than I thought I would, the real purpose of this letter is to apologize for the way our last conversation went. I can't be your wife, Brand, but I'd like to be your friend. If you can accept my friendship, then I'll be waiting to hear from you. If not, I'll understand.

Warm wishes,

Erin

Brand read through the letter twice before neatly folding it and replacing it inside the envelope. So she wanted to be friends.

He didn't. Not in the least.

He wasn't looking for a pal, a buddy, a sidekick. He wanted a wife, a woman who would stand at his side for the rest of his life. Someone to double the joy of the good times and divide the burden of the bad. When his ship pulled into port, he wanted her standing on the dock with the other wives and families, so eager to see him she'd be jumping up and down, hoping for a glimpse of him. When he walked down the gangplank, he wanted her to come rushing to his arms, unable to wait a second longer.

Erin wasn't offering him any of that. She had some milquetoast idea about them being pals. Well, he wanted no part of it. If she wanted a buddy, then she could look elsewhere.

Disgusted with the whole idea, Brand tossed her letter on his bunk. Erin MacNamera was going to have to offer him a whole lot more than friendship if she wanted any kind of relationship with him.

For a solid week, Erin rushed home from work to check her mail. She didn't try to fool herself by pretending she didn't care if Brand answered her letter or not. She did care, more than she wanted to admit. The way she figured it, he'd received her letter a week earlier. He'd take a few days to think matters over, and if everything went according to schedule, she'd have a letter back by the end of the following week.

No letter had arrived. At least not from Brand. Junk mail. Bills. Bank statements. They'd all made their way to Erin's address, but nothing from the one who mattered most.

"You might as well face it," she admonished herself. "He has no intention of answering your letter."

"What did you expect?" she asked herself a few minutes later. She knew what she'd expected. Letters. Hordes of them, filled, as they had been before, with humorous bits of wisdom that warmed her heart.

No such letters arrived. Not even a post-card.

Erin had never felt more melancholy in her life.

Erin's one-page letter had arrived exactly one month before. And for precisely thirty days Brand had been taking the letter out and reading it over again. Then he would methodically fold it and slip it back inside the envelope. After reading it so many times, he'd memorized every line.

At first keeping the letter was a show of strength on his part. He could hold it and touch a part of Erin. It felt good to be strong enough to stand his ground. He was unwilling to settle for second best with her. He wanted her heart . . . All right, he was willing to admit he needed more . . . He wanted her love for him to be so strong she was willing to relinquish everything. Frankly, he wasn't about to settle for anything less.

It was all or nothing, and that was the way it was meant to be. He was tired of going to her on bended knee. Tired of always being the one to compromise and give in. If anyone was going to make an effort to settle their differences, it would have to be Erin.

Besides, the way Brand figured it, Erin

needed this time apart to realize they were meant for each other. She'd had two months to forget they'd ever met, and apparently that hadn't worked. Hadn't she said she'd been trying to forget him? She'd also claimed it wasn't working. Brand figured he'd let time enhance his chances with his brown-eyed beauty. She was his, all right; she just had to figure that much out for herself.

Nevertheless, Brand watched the mail, hoping Erin would write him a second time. She wouldn't, but he couldn't keep from hoping.

It wasn't Erin he heard from, but her father.

Dear Brand:

I'm sorry I haven't written in a while, but you know me. I never was much good at writing, unless it's something important. This time it is. I owe you an apology. Forgive an old man, will you? I had no business setting you up with my daughter. That was my intent from the beginning, and I suspect you knew it. My Erin's a stubborn lass, and I thought if anyone could catch her eye, it would be your handsome face.

When I heard what happened, I wanted to shake that daughter of mine, but she's her own woman and she's got to make her own decisions, and her own mistakes.

I just never thought my Erin could be such a fool. I wrote and told her as much myself.

She isn't happy. That much I know for a fact. She has this friend, Aimee — you might have met her yourself. Apparently, Aimee and her husband have split, and so the two girls are in cahoots. To my way of thinking, no good's going to come of those two prowling around Seattle, looking for new relationships. Erin's a sweet thing, and I can't help worrying about her, although she wouldn't appreciate it if she knew. She'll do just fine. She's not as beautiful as some, but when she puts her mind to it, she'll find herself a catch that will make this old man proud. Frankly, the wife and I are looking forward to some grandchildren.

The last time we spoke, Erin mentioned she'd written you. Seems a shame things didn't work out between the two of you. A damn shame.

Keep in touch, will you? Give Romano and the others my regards.

Casey

Erin and Aimee were in cahoots? Brand definitely didn't like the sound of this. Not in the least. He read the letter a second time, and the not-so-subtle messages seemed to slap him in the face. Erin was unhappy and looking for a new relationship. If Aimee weren't involved, that fact wouldn't concern him nearly as much. Alone, Erin was a novice in the ways of attracting men, but with Aimee spurring her on, anything could happen.

Brand liked Aimee, he just wasn't sure he could trust her. The other woman had made a blatant effort to catch his eye that first afternoon when he'd followed Erin into the Blue Lagoon. He had the feeling that if he'd paid her the least bit of attention she would have run out of the place with her tail between her legs, but that wasn't what concerned him now. The fact that the two of them were out prowling around looking for action did trouble him.

Damn it all. This could ruin everything. Casey mentioning grandchildren hadn't helped matters, any, either. Damn it all, if Erin was going to be making love, it would be with him. If she was so keen on having children, then he'd be the one to father them, not some . . . stranger.

"I brought along something for us to drink," Aimee said as she walked in Erin's front door. "Friday night," she grumbled, "and we're reduced to renting movies."

"Don't complain. We're going to have a good time."

"Right." Erin carried a large bowl of popcorn into the living room, having to weave her way around the piano.

"I hope you rented something uplifting — something that's going to make us laugh and forget our troubles. You know, these might be difficult times for us, but we've got a whole lot to be grateful for."

"I do." Erin couldn't help but agree.

"By the way, what movies did you rent?"

Erin picked up the two videos and read the titles. "*Terms of Endearment* and *Beaches*."

Chapter Nine

July was half spent, and summer had yet to make an appearance in the Pacific Northwest. The skies had been overcast all afternoon, threatening rain. Erin had been running behind schedule most of the day and had gone directly from work to her Women in Transition class at South Seattle Community College.

By the time she arrived home, she was hungry and exhausted. By rote, she carried the mail into the house with her and set it on the counter as she searched the cupboards for something interesting for dinner. Chicken noodle soup was her best option, and she dumped the contents of the can into a saucepan and set it on the burner while she idly sorted through her mail.

The letter from Brand caught her unaware. For a moment all she could do was stare at it while her heart casually slipped into double time. Ripping open the envelope, her hands trembling, she slowly lowered herself into the cushioned chair and read.

Dearest Erin,
I kept telling myself I wouldn't write. Frankly, I was hoping the two of us could

start on fresh ground once I returned. I've discovered I can't wait. It was either write or go mad. Romano insists I give it one last shot. He's a friend of mine, and he knows your dad, too.

The last three months have been the longest of my life. I've always enjoyed sea duty, but not this time, not when matters between us have been left so unsettled.

All right, I'll admit it. I'm selfish and thoughtless, but damn it all, I love you. Believe me, I wish I didn't. I wish I could turn my back on you and walk away without a regret. I tried that, but it didn't work. Later, after you wrote, I reasoned I would give us both breathing room to settle matters in our own minds. That hasn't worked, either. And so what are we left with? Damned if I know.

I haven't a clue what's right anymore. I want another chance with you. If you're willing to give it a second shot, let me know. Only do it soon, would you? I'm about to go out of my mind.

Brand

Dearest Brand,
I don't know what's right anymore, either. All I do know is how wretched I feel ninety-nine percent of the time. I thought I could forget you, too, only it didn't work out that way. Believe me, I've tried.

Nothing seems to work. I'll be so glad when we can sit down and talk face-to-face. I've never felt like this.

You might remind your friend Romano that we have met. Obviously he doesn't remember. I attended his wedding with my mom and dad. It must have been ten years or so ago.

Write me again soon. I need to hear from you.

Erin

"What do you mean you've tried to forget me?" The sharp question was followed by an eerie long-distance hum that echoed in Erin's ear.

"Brand? Is that you?" The phone had woken her, and Erin hadn't yet had time to clear her thoughts. She brushed the hair out of her face and focused her gaze on the illuminated dial of her clock radio. It was the wee hours of the morning.

"Yes, it's me."

"Where are you?"

"Standing in some pay phone in the Philippines." His voice softened somewhat. "How are you?"

"Fine." Especially now that she'd heard his voice. It had taken her several seconds to ascertain that he was real and not part of the wildly romantic dreams she shared with him. She'd fantasized a hundred times talking to

Brand and woken hours later disillusioned by the knowledge that several thousand miles separated them. "How are you?"

"Fine. So you've tried to forget me."

"Yes . . . Oh, Brand, it's so good to talk to you." She scrambled to her knees, pressing the phone to her ear as if that would magically bring him closer. She felt like weeping, as nonsensical as it sounded. "I've been so miserable, and then you didn't write and didn't write and I swear I thought I was going crazy."

"Sweet heaven, Erin, I don't know what we're going to do. I wish to hell —" He was interrupted by someone in the background. Whoever it was seemed to be arguing with Brand.

"Brand?"

"Hold on, sweetheart. Romano's here, and he's giving me hell."

"Giving you hell! Why?"

Brand chuckled softly. "He seems to think it's important you know I've been behaving like a jealous idiot ever since I got your letter."

"You're jealous? Whatever for?" Erin found this piece of information nothing short of incredible. For all intents and purposes, she'd been living the life of a nun for three solid months.

Brand hesitated before explaining, "It all started when I heard from your dad. He told me Aimee and her husband had split up and that you two women had gone out on the prowl. Then your letter arrived, and you claimed you'd tried to forget me, and I put two and two together —"

"And came up with ten," Erin teased, having trouble hiding her delight. "Let me assure you, you don't have a thing to worry about."

"I can't help the way I feel," Brand admitted grudgingly. "No one's ever mattered to me as much as you. My mind got to wandering, and I couldn't help thinking . . . To make a long story short, I guess I've been a bit cross lately."

Once more the conversation was interrupted by Brand's friend. "All right, all right," Brand said. "According to half the men on the *Blue Ridge* I've been acting like a real bastard. Romano insisted I call you and find out exactly what's been going on before I jump to conclusions."

"Were you really jealous?" Erin still had a difficult time believing it.

"I already said I was," he snapped.

"If anyone should be worried, it's me. You're the one sailing to all those tropical islands. From what I remember, those native women are beautiful enough to turn any sailor's head."

"I swear to you, Erin, I haven't so much as spoken to a single woman since we left port.

How can I when all I think about is you?"

"Two and a half more months," she reminded him.

"I know. I can't remember any tour taking so long."

"Me either. I've got a couple of letters off to you this week, and I baked some chocolate chip cookies. Dad always loved it when Mom mailed him cookies. . . . I thought maybe you would too. Old habits die hard, I guess."

"I picked up something for you while we were in port, but I'd rather give it to you in person. Do you mind waiting?"

"No." But Erin noted that neither of them was willing to discuss how long it would be before they'd see each other again. Erin couldn't afford to fly off to Hawaii, especially after purchasing the piano. And Brand might not be able to get leave.

"Listen, Irish eyes, I've got to go."

"I know," she said, expelling a sigh of regret. "I'm so glad you phoned."

"I am, too. Write me."

"I will, I promise."

Yet both were reluctant to hang up the line until Erin heard Romano arguing with Brand in the background.

"Hey, Face, aren't you going to tell her you love her?"

Romano's question was followed by a short pause before Brand said, "She already knows."

Smiling to herself, Erin relaxed and grinned sheepishly. Yes, she did know, but it wouldn't have done any harm to have heard him tell her one more time.

Dearest Erin,
The cookies arrived today. You never told me you could bake like this. They're fabulous. I can't tell you how much it means to me that you'd send me cookies.

I don't know what the men think of me. For the first part of the cruise I was an ill-tempered bear, snapping at everyone. These days I walk around wearing a silly grin, passing out cookies like a first-grade teacher to her favorite pupils.

By the way, you haven't mentioned the piano lately. Did you know I play? My mother forced me to take lessons for five years. I hated it then but have had reason to be grateful since.

I'm sorry this is so short, but the mail's due to be picked up anytime and I wanted to get this off so you'd know how much I appreciate the cookies.

Miss you,

Brand

P.S. The next time you write, send me your picture.

"Well?" Erin asked for the third time as Aimee reviewed the stack of snapshots. Brand had been hounding her for weeks for a photo. She'd tried to put him off, explaining that she really didn't take a good picture, but he wouldn't listen, claiming that if she didn't send one he'd write and ask her family for a photo. It didn't take much thinking on her part to realize that her dad would take delight in sending off a whole series of pictures, no doubt starting with naked baby shots. "Which one is the best?"

Aimee shrugged laconically. "They're all about the same."

"I know, but which one makes me look sexy and glamorous and every lieutenant's dream?"

Aimee's questioning gaze rose steadily to meet Erin's. "He asked for *your* picture, you know, not one of Madonna in her brass-tipped bra."

"I realize that, but I wanted something special, something that made me look attractive."

"You are attractive."

"More than attractive," Erin added sheepishly. "Sexy."

"Erin, sweetheart, at the risk of offending you, I'd like to remind you we took these photos with my camera, which cost all of forty dollars. If you're looking for someone to airbrush the finish, you should have contacted a professional."

"It's just that —"

"Hey, sweetie, you don't need to explain anything to me."

Erin knew she didn't, but she couldn't help feeling a twinge of guilt. Aimee's divorce was progressing smoothly enough. Matters, however, were starting to heat up now that the attorneys were involved.

"So have you heard from the sailor boy lately?" Aimee asked with a hint of sarcasm. She sorted through the pictures again and selected three, setting them aside. Falling in love wasn't a subject that interested Aimee these days. The divorce was proving to be far more painful than she'd ever expected.

"He writes often."

"And you?"

"I . . . I write often, too."

"How much longer before he's back in Hawaii?"

Erin had it figured out right down to the number of hours, although it would do her little good. "About six weeks."

Aimee nodded, but Erin wasn't completely sure her friend had even heard her.

"This one," Aimee said unexpectedly, handing her the snapshot. Erin was standing in front of a rosebush in her yard, where all of the photos had been taken.

She was wearing a dress in a soft shade of olive green, which nicely complemented her coloring. Her sleeves were rolled up past her elbow, and a narrow row of buttons ran down the length of the front. The outfit was complemented by a woven belt and a matching large-brimmed hat that shaded her face.

"This one. Really?" Erin questioned. It wasn't the one she would have chosen. Her eyes were lowered, unlike in the other photos, and her mouth was curved slightly upward in a subtle smile.

"He'll love it," Aimee insisted.

Dearest Erin,
The picture arrived in today's letter. I'd forgotten how beautiful you are. I couldn't take my eyes off you. It made me miss you so much more than I do already. An empty feeling came over me. One so big an earthmover couldn't fill it. I don't know how to explain it. I'm not sure I can.

All I know is I love you so much it frightens me. Somehow, someway, we're going to come up with a solution to all this. We have to. I can't bear to think of not having you in my life.

I'm sorry to hear about Aimee and her husband and hope they can patch things up.

And no, I haven't seen any women in grass skirts lately. Haven't you figured it out yet, my sweet Irish rose? I only have eyes for you.

Love,

Brand

Brand taped Erin's picture to the wall next to his berth. He'd seen other guys do the same thing and had never understood what led mature men to do something so juvenile. Now he understood. Love did. The last person he saw when he went to sleep at night was Erin, and she was the first one to greet him each morning. Sometimes he'd linger a few moments extra just staring at her.

He loved the picture. Just the way she was standing with her back to the sun, bright shreds of light folding golden arms around her. Her eyes were downcast, and she had the look of a woman longing to be kissed.

Brand ran his tongue around the outside of his lips. It had been so long since he'd kissed Erin he'd almost forgotten what it was like.

Almost forgotten.

What he did remember was enough to prompt a pronounced tightness in his pants. Although she was wearing a very proper olive-green dress in the snapshot, the image of her standing in the sunlight reminded him of the morning she'd wandered into the kitchen in her flannel gown. She'd smelled of lavender and musk, and the yoke of her prim gown had been embroidered in satin threads that emphasized her perky breasts. Erin had beautiful breasts, and the sudden need Brand experienced to taste and feel them was enough to produce a harsh groan. His breath fled. It was time to take a cold shower, something he seemed to be doing a lot of lately. He pressed his fingers to his lips and then bounced them against Erin's picture, doubting that she had a clue how crazy he was about her.

Dear Erin,
You don't know me. At least I don't think we've ever met. I'm Ginger Romano. My husband, Alex, and Brand Davis are both aboard the *Blue Ridge*. By now you've probably heard about Brand's promotion. He's been promoted to full-grade lieu-tenant.

Brand's real popular with the guys, and they wanted to do something special for him. That's why Alex wrote me about you. A few of Brand's friends decided to get together and throw a surprise party for him to celebrate his promotion.

Someone thought it might be fun if they hired a woman to jump out of a cake. That's when Alex came up with a much better idea. They're going to throw that party, and there's going to be a woman

200

there all right, but we want to surprise him with *you*. Everyone went together and pitched in and we have enough for your airplane ticket. You're welcome to stay at the house here with Alex and me, if you don't mind kids. We have three, and they're a handful, but the welcome mat's out and we'd really be pleased if you could.

Let me know at your earliest opportunity if it's the least bit feasible for you to arrive the second week of October. We'll need to know soon, though, so we can book your flight. Please remember this is a surprise.

I'm looking forward to meeting you.

Sincerely,

Ginger Romano

"You're going?" Aimee asked again, as if she still couldn't believe Erin had agreed to this crazy, spur-of-the-moment plan. "You're honestly going?"

Maybe it was a crazy thing to do, but Erin couldn't resist. She could never have afforded the airplane ticket herself, and this seemed her golden opportunity to spend time with Brand. They'd been apart so many months, and they'd trudged over a mountain range of emotions and doubts.

She had his picture, but she wasn't exactly

201

sure she remembered what he looked like. He'd contacted her by phone only one time in the last six months. Was she flying to him? In a heartbeat!

"I'm going," she assured Aimee, tucking her curling iron in her suitcase.

"I don't suppose you need a friend to tag along for moral support?"

"I do, but I can't afford you," Erin joked.

"Don't worry, I can't afford me, either. Apparently no one can, not even Steve." She was trying to make light of the facts with a joke, but it fell flat.

"Don't worry," Erin promised, "I'll be back in time for the settlement hearing. I won't let you go through this alone."

Aimee's eyes filled with appreciation. "Thanks. I'm counting on you." She glanced around the bedroom one last time. "Well, it looks like you've got everything under control." Aimee made it sound like a sharp contrast to her own life, and Erin struggled with a sudden twinge of guilt.

"Hey," Aimee said with a short, pathetic laugh, "don't look so woebegone. It isn't every day you get an opportunity like this. Enjoy it while you can. Play in the sun, relax, stroll along the beach. I'll be fine . . . You don't need to worry about little ol' me."

"Aimee!"

"All right, all right, I'm being ridiculous. I do want you to have fun. It's just that I'm going to miss you something terrible."

"I'm going to miss you, too, but it's only a week."

Erin glanced around one last time to be sure she'd packed everything she needed. Aimee was driving her to the airport and dropping her off. In less than two hours she'd be boarding the flight. Several hours later, she'd step off the Boeing 747 in Honolulu, where Ginger would be waiting to pick her up. She'd be leaving the cold rain of Seattle behind and disembarking in balmy eighty-degree sunshine.

Not a bad trade.

The flight seemed to take an eternity. Several times Erin had to pinch herself to make sure all this was real. She felt like a game-show winner who hadn't expected anything more than the consolation prize. Yet here she was flying to Brand with seven uninterrupted days of heaven stretching out in front of her.

The *Blue Ridge* was due to sail into Pearl Harbor sometime late Wednesday afternoon. The party was scheduled for Thursday evening. Ginger had taken care of most of the details, along with a couple of other navy wives and Lieutenant Commander Catherine Fredrickson, another of Brand's friends. For the past month, Erin had been corresponding with Ginger, and she liked her immensely.

The hardest part was keeping the fact that

Erin was in Hawaii a secret until Thursday evening.

"I don't know where the hell she could be," Brand told Romano Thursday morning. "I tried phoning every hour all night. She didn't mention she was going away."

"Maybe something came up."

"Obviously," he barked. Brand was in a sour mood. For days he'd been looking forward to phoning Erin. It was the first thing he'd done when he'd walked into his apartment. The anticipation of hearing her voice was the only thing that had gotten him through those last few weeks. Rarely had he ever been more restless or more ready for a tour to end.

Each night for three weeks he'd dreamed of listening to the soft catch in her voice when she realized it was him on the line. For the first time in six hellish months he could speak to her freely without someone standing over his shoulder the way Alex had in the Philippines. He hoped that when they spoke this time they might accomplish something.

At the very least they could discuss what they had to do to see each other again.

For several long months he'd thought of little else but being with Erin again. Yet, when the time arrived, she was gone. Vanished. No one seemed to know where she was.

Brand had gone so far as to contact her family. Casey didn't sound the least bit concerned, claiming Erin often had to travel out of town on business trips. But, now that Brand mentioned it, Casey did seem to remember Erin saying something about flying off to Spokane sometime soon.

If that was the case, she hadn't bothered to tell Brand.

"How about going out for a couple of beers?" Romano suggested late that same afternoon.

"Ginger's going to let you?" he asked disbelievingly.

"She won't care. Bobby's at soccer practice, and frankly, what she doesn't know won't hurt her."

Brand didn't know what had gotten into his friend. Usually Alex couldn't wait to get home to his family, and once he was back, he spent plenty of time with the youngsters. Brand had always admired the fact Romano was a good family man. He hoped when the time came he'd be as conscientious a husband and father.

Brand considered his options. It was either hang around his apartment all night, hoping Erin would contact him, or visit the Officers' Club and talk shop with a few old friends. The second option was by far the most appealing, yet something elemental tugged at his heart. He hated the thought he might miss Erin, if she should happen to call.

"Well?" Romano pressed impatiently. "What's your choice?"

"I don't suppose one beer would hurt."

A twinkling light flashed in Alex's sea green eyes. "Nope, I don't think it will, either."

As soon as Brand had fastened his seat belt, Romano started the engine and drove past the Officers' Club and outside the navy compound. "Hey, where are we going?"

"For a beer," Alex reminded him, doing his best to hide a grin.

Something was up. Brand might not have a whole lot to do with Navy intelligence, but he didn't need a master's degree in human nature to determine that something was awry.

"All right, Romano," Brand insisted, "tell me what's going on here."

"What makes you think anything is?"

"Let's start with the fact you're free the second night we're in port?"

"All right, all right, if you must know, the guys went together and planned a small party in your honor, *Lieutenant* Davis."

Amused, Brand chuckled. He should have known a long time before now that his friends wouldn't let that pass without making some kind of fuss. "Who's in on this?"

"Just about everyone. Only . . ."

"Only what?"

"There's one small problem, if you want to

call it that." Romano hesitated. "It's a little bit embarrassing, but the guys wanted to make this special, so they hired a woman."

"They did what?" Brand demanded.

"Someone got the bright idea that it would be fun to see your face if they rolled in a cake and had a woman leap out of the top."

Brand slowly shook his head. "I certainly hope you're kidding."

"Sorry, I'm not. I couldn't talk them out of it."

Brand set his hand over his eyes and slowly shook his head. He should be amused by all this. "A woman?"

"You got it, buddy."

Brand mulled over the information and chuckled. There wasn't much he could do about it now, but he appreciated the warning. "Whatever happens, don't ever let Erin find out about it, understand?"

"You've got my word of honor."

The Cliff House was a restaurant with a reputation for excellent food and an extensive list of imported wine. Brand was mildly surprised that the establishment would sanction the type of entertainment his friends had planned.

The receptionist smiled warmly when Romano announced Brand's name, and she gingerly led them to a banquet room off the main dining room.

"Hey, you guys went all out," Brand muttered under his breath as they followed the petite Chinese woman.

"Nothing but the best," Romano assured him, still grinning.

Several shouts and cheers of welcome went out when the two men walked into the room. Brand was handed a bottle of imported German beer and a basket of thick pretzels and led to a table in the front of the room.

"Are you ready to be entertained?" Romano asked, claiming the empty chair beside him. He reached for a bowl of mixed nuts and leaned back, eager for the show.

Brand nodded. He might as well get this over with first thing and be done with it. He forced a smile and a relaxed pose while two of the crewmen from the *Blue Ridge* rolled out a six-foot-tall box tied up with a large red bow. It wasn't a cake, but close enough.

"You're supposed to untie the ribbon," Romano explained, urging him forward.

Reluctantly Brand stood and walked up to the front of the room. There must have been fifty men — and several women — all standing around, intently watching him. He tried to act nonchalant, as if he did this sort of thing every day.

He lifted one end of the broad red ribbon and tugged, expecting it to fall open. It didn't, and he was offered loud bits of advice by the men on the floor.

Brand tried a second time, tugging harder.

The ribbon fell away, and the four sides of the box lazily folded open. Brand wasn't exactly sure what he expected. His mind filled with several possibilities for which he was mentally prepared. But what did appear left him speechless with shock.

"Hello, Brand," Erin greeted with a warm smile as she stepped forward. She was wearing the same olive-green dress as in the picture she'd sent. For a wild moment, Brand was convinced she was a figment of his imagination. She had to be.

"Say something," Romano shouted. "Don't just stand there looking like a bump on a log."

"Erin?"

Her brown eyes had never been wider. "You're disappointed?"

"Sweet heaven, no," he groaned, reaching for her, dragging her into the shelter of his arms.

Chapter Ten

Brand blinked, unable to believe Erin was so soft against his body. Perhaps he was hallucinating. All the lonely months they'd spent apart might have dulled his senses. Was he so desperate for her that his mind had mystically forced her to materialize?

Brand didn't know, but he was about to find out. In a heartbeat, his mouth came crashing down on hers. She was real. More real than he dared remember. Soft. Sweet. And in his arms.

Low, guttural sounds made their way up his throat as he slanted his mouth over hers. The men behind him were hooting and cheering, but Brand barely heard them above Erin's small cry of welcome.

He felt the tears slide down her face, and he loved her so much that it was all he could do not to break down and weep himself. He kissed her again, sliding his tongue along hers, deep, deeper, into the honey-sweet depths of her mouth.

The boisterous shouts from behind him reminded Brand that, no matter how much he wanted to, he couldn't continue to make love to Erin. At least not in front of several dozen of his peers. Pulling away from her was the hardest thing he'd ever done.

"Are you surprised?" Romano teased, joining him in the front of the room and slapping him hard across the back.

Unable to speak, Brand nodded. His eyes, insatiable and greedy, locked with Erin's. He couldn't resist hugging her once more. Wrapping his arms around her, he closed his eyes and breathed in the scent of lavender and musk that was hers alone. He'd dreamed of this moment so often and now it was all coming to pass, and he couldn't believe it was happening.

He gazed into the sea of faces watching him, unable to express the gratitude in his heart.

"Come on, Lieutenant," Catherine Fredrickson instructed, "sit down before you make a fool of yourself. Dinner's about to be served." He and Catherine had worked together for nearly four years, and he was an admirer of hers. Their relationship was probably a little unusual, when he thought about it. Catherine was a friend, and he'd never thought of her as anything more. It worried him that Erin might feel threatened by the lieutenant commander.

"We brought out the dessert early," another friend teasingly called out to him.

Keeping Erin close to his side, Brand led the way to their table. Several friends came forward, eager to introduce themselves to

Erin. Many had worked with her father at one time or another and were interested in news of the fun-loving Casey MacNamera.

No matter how many people spoke to him, or commanded his attention, Brand couldn't take his eyes off his beautiful Irish miss for more than a few seconds. His gaze was magnetically drawn back to her again and again.

Erin's gaze seemed equally hungry. A myriad of emotions scored Brand, many of which he couldn't have identified. All he knew, all he wanted to know, was that Erin was sitting at his side. His heart swelled with a love so strong that it made him weak.

Men gathered around him. Friends asked him questions. Dinner was served. Brand laughed, talked, ate and did everything else that was required of him. But every now and again his eyes would slide to Erin's, and they'd nearly drown in each other's presence.

She was even more beautiful than he remembered. Not so strikingly attractive that her loveliness called attention to herself, but her rare inner quality of strength and gentleness shone through.

"How long have you known about this?" he whispered, twining their fingers.

"A month." She smiled shyly. "The longest month of my life."

"Mine, too." He braced his forehead against hers and breathed in the warm scent of her. It was in his mind, then and there, to tell her how much he loved and needed her. But emotion constricted the muscles of his throat, making speech difficult.

"Here," Romano said, slapping a set of keys on the tabletop.

Brand didn't understand.

"Take the car," he instructed.

"Your car? But how will you get home?" Brand realized his speech was too sporadic to make sense.

"Ginger," Romano answered with a chuckle. "Now get out of here before someone gives you a reason to stay."

Brand didn't need a second invitation. He stood, his fingers linked with Erin's. He took a long detour around the room, shaking hands with his comrades, wanting to thank his friends for the biggest — and by far the best — surprise of his life.

When he'd finished, he walked purposefully out of the restaurant.

"Oh, Brand . . ." Erin whispered once they were alone together. She seemed at a loss to continue.

Brand understood. For weeks he'd been planning what he wanted to say to her. His intention was to logically, intellectually lead her to the conclusion that they should do as he'd suggested months earlier and marry. He planned to tackle each one of her objections with sound reasoning and irrefutable logic. But every word he'd prepared sailed straight into the sunset without ever reaching his lips. All that mattered to Brand in that moment was holding her, loving her.

He gently brought her into his arms and buried his face in the delicate curve of her neck. Brand felt the series of quivers that racked her shoulders and moved down her spine. He pulled her flush against him in an effort to comfort her. Her tears dampened his neck, and her warm breath fanned his throat.

Holding her this close was torment of another kind. Her soft breasts caressed his hard chest, and her stomach was flattened against his. All torture should be this incredibly sweet, he reasoned.

He laid his hand on her hair, filled his fingers with it, savoring the silky smoothness of the thick auburn tresses.

"Let's get out of here," Brand whispered when he could endure the pleasure of holding her no longer.

"Where?"

If they went back to his place, there was no question in his mind that she'd spend the night in his bed. No doubt Romano and the others assumed that was exactly what would happen. Maybe Erin was thinking the same thing herself. He didn't know.

His heart and body were greedy for her. But his need wasn't so voracious that it blocked out sound judgment. He wanted

Erin as his lover, but sharing a bed with her wasn't nearly enough to satisfy him. If he was looking for sexual gratification, he could find that with any number of women.

He yearned for much more from Erin. He wanted her for his wife, and he wasn't willing to settle for anything less.

Brand helped her into the car. He noted when he started the engine that Erin's hands were clenched together in her lap. She was nervous. A slow smile worked its way across his mouth. What the hell, he was as tense as she was. Only in his case he was too sophisticated to show it.

"Where are we going?" she asked in a voice so small he could scarcely make out the words.

"The beach."

She relaxed at that, tucking her hand under his arm and leaning her head on his shoulder as he steered the car out of the parking lot. The warm, soothing wind whipped past them as Brand drove the narrow, twisting road down the steep hillside. Palm trees swayed in the breeze, and the silver light of a full moon reflected against the crashing waves of the surf.

Walking hand in hand down the sandy embankment, Brand led the way toward the water. The night was warm and the beach empty.

Brand paused once they reached the ocean,

faced her and wrapped his arms around her trim waist, holding on to her. Her eyes met his, and he read the confusion and the doubts. Now wasn't the time for either.

"There's so much I planned to tell you," Erin murmured, seeming to search for the right words to say to him.

"Later," he whispered before his mouth met hers. "We have all the time in the world to straighten out our problems. For now, love me."

She moaned and slipped her arms up his chest, leaning into him as she gave him her mouth. Their kiss was like spontaneous combustion, their need for each other fierce and compelling. His tongue breached the barrier of her lips and plundered deep and long. All ten of his fingers sank into her hair as their kisses, tempered with tenderness, delved deeper and deeper. Sweeter than anything Brand had ever known. Slowly he ran his hands over her shoulders and the sides of her waist to her hips, finally cupping her buttocks. He drew her up slightly until her abdomen settled naturally over the hard imprint of his growing need. For an elongated second neither of them moved. Then Erin, his sweet, innocent Erin, started to rub against him, creating a hot friction, a burning need, that all but devoured him. Each sway of her hips, each rotation, eradicated every shred of reason Brand possessed.

"Ah, Erin," he rasped. Feverishly he tore his mouth from hers, hoping the cool air would clear his head. But it did little to help.

Her mouth. Her sweet, delectable mouth tasted even better than he'd fantasized. He couldn't seem to taste enough of her, and each kiss only quickened his appetite for more.

Even through the thick fabric of her dress he could feel her nipples harden. Her breasts felt lush and full, pressed as they were against his chest. Ripe. He remembered how they felt in his hands, how they'd filled his palms, spilled over. Unable to resist, his thumbs skirted over her nipples.

She moaned softly as his fingers fumbled with the row of buttons until the first several were free. He slipped the top partway down her shoulders and was challenged by her teddy and bra.

"Are so many clothes necessary?" he moaned, then alternated his attention from one breast to the other, his mouth closing over the material, making wet circles in the satin.

"Yes, all these clothes are necessary," she whispered, and he could hear the laughter in her voice.

He wanted her. Then. There. His need was so great that a thin film of sweat broke out over his body. Brand closed his eyes and gnashed his teeth in an effort to rein in the desire that coursed through him like liquid fire, gathering inevitably in his loins.

Erin stepped away from him and slowly, purposefully, unfastened the buttons of her dress, letting it slip to the sand.

"W-what are you doing?" Dear sweet heaven, she was going to make this impossible.

She smiled boldly up at him. "Let's swim."

Brand was about to remind her that neither of them had a suit when she started running toward the water.

"Erin," he called after her, and at the same moment he sank to the sand and started unlacing his shoes. Five years in Hawaii and he'd never once done anything so crazy. She was out in the surf, splashing away like a dolphin, and he was struggling to remove his pants, which he sent flying into the night. Without bothering to unbutton his shirt, he slipped it over his head, balled it in his fist and impatiently hurled it down on the beach.

By the time he joined her, Erin was waist-deep in the surf, holding her arms out to him. "Come in, Lieutenant, the water's fine."

"If you'd wanted to swim, I'd have preferred to wait until I had on a suit, and not a double-breasted one."

"I'm double-breasted," she teased, leaping up and down in the water like a porpoise to give him a tantalizing view of her breasts. Brand was certain she had no idea how much she was revealing. When wet, the white satin material of her bra was as transparent as glass. She might as well be nude for all the cover her underthings afforded her.

With unhurried strides, Brand walked toward her. The tide slapped against his long legs, but he refused to pause, his pace uniform and steady.

"Besides," she added with a taunting grin. "We both needed to cool off, don't you agree?"

"I had everything under control."

"No, you didn't, and neither did I." She rubbed her hands up and down her arms as a tiny shiver went through her.

"This craziness is supposed to cool us off?" he muttered under his breath. If anything, Brand was hotter than ever. Her nipples had beaded, the dark aureoles pointing directly at him, commanding his attention. The ends of her hair were wet and dripping lazily onto her smooth shoulders. The salt water rolled down her creamy white neck and into the valley between her breasts. Everything seemed to point in that direction, including his gaze.

When she was a few yards away from him, Erin floated into his arms. Her body was warm and slippery as she locked her arms around his neck, and her long legs folded over his hips. The instant her weight settled against him, she felt the strength of him.

Slowly she raised her soft gaze to his, and her eyes widened slightly.

"Brand?"

"As you can see, your plans have backfired, my dear."

"Now what?"

She shifted her weight slightly, scooting her derriere over the protrusion, and in the process nearly unmanned him. She was too innocent to understand what she was doing to him. If this continued much longer, they'd end up making love while standing waist-deep in the surf.

"Let me taste you," he pleaded, his voice low and guttural.

As though in a trance, Erin nodded. She reached back and unfastened her bra. Her breasts fell free of the restraining material and settled against the water-slicked planes of his chest. Her nipples, pouting prettily, felt so hot, so gloriously wonderful against his cool skin, that for a second he forgot to breathe.

She must have felt it, too, because her breath caught softly then. Clenching handfuls of his hair, she began to move, circling her breasts against him, creating a delicious, indescribable friction.

"Oh, baby," he groaned as he lifted her higher, sliding his open mouth across her breasts, creating a slick trail, sucking lightly from one breast and then the other, loving the taste of her. His mouth closed around her, and he gloried in the untamed eagerness of her response.

Her hands were in his hair, and she was making low whimpering sounds. He languidly paid attention to each breast, rolling his tongue around the passion-beaded nipple, sucking strongly, then gentling the action.

Between sighs and moans Erin encouraged him to take more and more of her into his mouth, her voice soft and trembling as she pleaded, rotating her hips against him, her feet digging into the small of his back.

Brand had reached the limit of his endurance. "Erin," he begged, "Oh, baby, hold still . . . please."

"No . . . oh, Brand, I . . . don't think I can . . . It feels so good."

"I know, baby, I know. Too good."

She gently thrashed against him. "Kiss me," she whispered.

Brand willingly complied. Her mouth opened under the force of his, and her tongue met his in joyous union. The slow, smooth gyration of her hips against him caused the blood to rush to his head until he feared he would lose his footing. He felt as powerless against Erin as he was against the flow of the tide.

His hand slipped inside the wide leg of her tap pants and over her bare derriere. Then, slowly, gradually, he slipped his fingers toward the warm, moist opening of her womanhood. She opened to him like a rosebud responding to the warming rays of the sun. Her pulsating warmth closed around him, and she started to whimper as he gently claimed possession of the innermost part of her body.

Making panting sounds, Erin squeezed her eyes closed and began to move against him, her actions countering his. Her nails dug deep into the thick muscles of his shoulders, but he felt no discomfort as her mouth hungrily latched on to his, her tongue boldly searching out his. He felt her climax and sensed the pulsating waves of undiluted pleasure as she relaxed heavily against him.

Gradually, her eyes opened, and their gazes held for a long moment. Brand loved her so much that he thought his pounding heart would explode in his chest. She smiled at him. Shyly. Almost apologetically. Her look was so tender that he could have drowned in it.

The sound of laughter coming from behind them on the shore brought Brand rudely back to reality.

"There are people coming," Erin whispered in a panic.

"I told you before this isn't such a good idea."

"But . . . Brand, I'm nearly naked."

"For all intents and purposes, you are indeed naked."

"Do something."

"You're joking."

"We can't just stand here."

"Why not? With any luck they'll stroll past and not notice two crazy people lolling around in the surf. Forget it, they'll notice."

Erin expelled a sharp breath and pressed her forehead against Brand's. "This is all my fault."

"I know," he whispered, kissing her soundly. "But I forgive you." He hugged her close, amused. Her face was beet red; even her breasts were rosy with embarrassment. He waited until the sound of voices had faded, and then he carried Erin effortlessly back onto the beach.

Erin was in the kitchen with Ginger Romano, slicing pineapple into a large stainless-steel bowl for a fresh fruit salad they were making for the evening meal. Ginger was shaping hamburger patties, pressing the meat firmly together between the palms of her hands.

"You're quiet this afternoon," Ginger said, smiling warmly in Erin's direction. The two had been standing side by side for the past ten minutes without a word passing between them. The silence, however, was a comfortable one. Erin and Ginger had become fast friends in the past few days.

For the first time that afternoon the house

223

was relatively quiet. The two youngest Romano children were napping. Alex and Brand had taken six-year-old Bobby to the grocery store with them to buy charcoal briquettes for the barbecue.

Erin smiled lazily over at her friend. "I don't mean to be so uncommunicative. I was just thinking, I guess." She was due to leave Oahu in two short days. She didn't want to go. Seattle was her home, and she loved living in the Pacific Northwest, but she'd forgotten how beautiful Hawaii could be.

"Who are you trying to kid?" Erin muttered under her breath. It wasn't Hawaii she found so relaxing and stimulating. It was being with Brand.

"Did you say something?" Ginger asked.

"Not really . . . I sometimes talk to myself."

"I do that myself when I'm thinking. Usually I do it when something's worrying me."

"I was just wondering what's going to become of me and Brand." No one had said anything, but Erin couldn't shake the feeling that everyone was waiting for them to announce their wedding plans. The pressure was there; it was low-key and subtle, but nevertheless Erin could feel it as strongly as she'd felt the tide against her legs when in the ocean.

"I take it you've enjoyed yourself this

week?" Ginger asked, setting the plate of hamburger patties aside.

"Everyone's been wonderful."

"You've been quite a hit yourself. We were all eager to meet you."

"In other words," Erin said with a teasing smile, "Brand's friends were more curious than generous when it came to sending me that airplane ticket."

"Exactly! I do hope you enjoyed this week in Hawaii."

"What's there not to enjoy?" Erin teased.

"Then you might consider moving here," she suggested boldly.

"No way." Erin was quick to discount the suggestion. "Seattle's home."

"Have you lived there long?"

"Two years. I graduated from the University of Texas, but spent the first two years in Florida before transferring."

"You did your graduate work in Texas, too?"

"No, I finished up in New York, so you can see why I'm happy to settle in Seattle at last. It's my first home, and I intend to stay put for a good long while."

"I can understand that," Ginger said thoughtfully. "You were certainly a hit. We're going to be sorry to see you go."

"I passed muster, then?"

"With flying colors. It does my heart good to see the mighty Brandon Davis fall in love.

I was beginning to doubt it would ever happen. He's such a stubborn cuss. He'd date a woman for a few weeks, then lose interest and drop her. I knew from the moment he mentioned your name, you were different, and so did everyone else."

"Brand is special." She licked the juice from her fingers and set the paring knife in the sink. "Frankly, I can't help worrying that I'm simply more of a challenge to him than the other women he's dated. I'm not like the others. I refused to fall at his feet." Although she attempted to make light of the fact, she considered it the bona fide truth.

"I don't think that's it, exactly," Ginger countered quickly. She paused and leaned her hip against the counter. "In some ways, perhaps, but not completely. Now that I've gotten to know you, I can understand why Brand's so enthralled with you. You two complement each other. You seem to balance each other. Brand's outgoing, you're a little withdrawn. Not unsociable — don't misunderstand me. Brand's one hundred percent Navy —"

"I'm one hundred percent not."

Ginger paused, and her smooth brow pleated in a frown. "It really troubles you, doesn't it?"

Erin nodded. "If I hadn't grown up around the military, I probably would naively accept this lifestyle as part of what it means to love

Brand. But I've been there. The navy expects certain concessions from a wife and family, and frankly, I refuse to make those. I'm a navy brat, and I know what it means to marry a man in the military. It's one of life's cruel practical jokes that I'd meet Brand this way and fall for him."

"I don't look at it that way," Ginger said, scooting out a stool and sitting down. "Before I married Alex, I thought long and hard about accepting his proposal. I wasn't keen on marrying a navy man, knowing from the first that I would always place second in his life."

"Exactly," Erin agreed, but it was so much more than that. If she did marry Brand, her life would no longer be her own.

"I prefer to think of Alex and myself as a team. We're contributors to the defense and security of our country. I'm proud of Alex and the role he plays, but I'm equally satisfied with my own contribution. If it weren't for my talents, my enthusiasm, my dedication, and that of the other wives and families, the navy would lose its effectiveness. I realize I sound like a propaganda machine, but frankly, it's the truth."

"I grew up hearing and believing all that." Erin straightened and ceremoniously squared her shoulders, keeping her eyes trained straight ahead. In a monotone, she recited what she could remember of the Navy

Wifeline creed. "I believe that through better understanding of the navy, wives will enjoy and accept more enthusiastically the navy way of life, and we pledge our efforts . . . Blah, blah, blah."

"You do know it," Ginger said with a smile.

"For eighteen years I was part and parcel of the demanding tempo of navy life. I was uprooted more times than I can remember. I've lived on more bases than some admirals. It was one move after another, and frankly, I don't know if I'm willing to make that kind of sacrifice a second time."

Erin was being as honest as she knew how to be. Yes, she loved Brand, loved him with all her heart, but being in love didn't solve the problem.

"What are you going to do?"

"I don't know," she whispered, suddenly miserable.

Things had changed between Brand and Erin after their night on the beach. Never again had either of them allowed their love-making to progress to that level.

They spent every available moment together, but they did little more than kiss and hold hands. Although she'd seen the tourist attractions a number of times before, Brand escorted Erin all over the island. It was as though they both needed to see and appreciate the beauty and the splendor of Oahu through one another's eyes.

"I wish I knew what I could say that would help you," Ginger said, crossing her legs. She folded her arms around her middle and stared into space. "The thing that impresses me most about you and Brand is that it's like the two of you have been married for years and years. You seem to read one another's thoughts. It's uncanny. Forgive me for saying this, but it's almost as if you were meant to be together."

"It isn't as dramatic as you think," Erin argued. "I know the way a man in the navy thinks."

And behaves. Brand wasn't fooling her any. They hadn't talked once about the very subject that had driven them apart. Brand was biding his time, waiting until her defenses were lowered and she was weakest. His game plan was one Erin recognized well from her own father's school of strategy. Brand assumed that if he let matters follow a natural progression, things would work out his way. He seemed to believe that once she was head over heels in love with him, the fact he was navy wouldn't matter.

Wrong. It mattered a whole lot. Only she didn't want to spend their first time together in six months arguing. Apparently Brand didn't, either, and so the subject was one they'd both avoided. Brand by design. Erin . . .

she didn't know. For selfish reasons, she guessed.

The front door opened, followed by the sound of running feet. "Mommy, we're home." Six-year-old Bobby burst into the kitchen like a pistol shot.

Brand and Alex followed closely behind. Alex carried a large bag of briquettes.

Slipping up behind Erin, Brand wrapped his arms around her waist and kissed her cheek. "Did you miss me?"

"Dreadfully."

"That's what I hoped." He smiled wickedly and turned her around to reward her with a kiss. The intensity caught Erin off guard.

When Brand released her, his eyes held hers. "We need some time alone."

She nodded. The following afternoon she was scheduled to return to Seattle. The day of reckoning had arrived.

Erin was barely able to down her dinner. The four adults sat around the picnic table, lingering over their coffee, while the three youngsters ran wild in the backyard.

"Hawaii is beautiful this time of year," Erin remarked lazily, catching Brand's eye.

He slipped her hand into his and squeezed tightly. "It's beautiful any time of year." His look suggested they make their excuses, but Erin wasn't falling into his game plan quite so easily.

She stood and carried Brand's and her

plate into the kitchen, rinsing them off and stacking them in the dishwasher.

"You've been quiet this afternoon," Brand commented, sticking their iced-tea glasses in the top rack. "Is something troubling you?"

She nodded sadly. "I don't want to leave you." It plagued her more than she dared admit. She couldn't stay. Seattle was her home, not Hawaii. Her house and her piano awaited her return. As did Aimee and her job.

Brand reached for her shoulders, turning her toward him. His eyes were hot and fervent as they stared into hers. "Then don't go back."

"It's not that simple," Erin protested.

"Why isn't it?"

Frantic for an excuse, Erin said the first thing that came to mind. "Because of Catherine Fredrickson."

"What the hell has she got to do with anything?" Brand demanded harshly.

Chapter Eleven

"Catherine's in love with you."

Brand stared at Erin stupidly, as if he weren't certain he'd heard her correctly. His expression was first astonished and then incredulous. "What the hell are you talking about? As I recall, the conversation went something along the lines that you didn't want to leave Hawaii, to which I had the simple solution. Don't go. As I recall, Catherine's name didn't once enter the conversation."

"She's in love with you."

"She's not, and even if she was, what has that got to do with anything?" Brand demanded, holding tight reins on his patience. He glanced over his shoulder as if he feared Alex or Ginger might make an appearance. Plainly the subject was one he didn't want them listening in on.

"It's . . . something a woman likes to know when she's interested in a man herself."

Brand made a harsh sound that was a groan of abject frustration.

"I . . . I think you should marry her." Erin thought nothing of the sort, but said so for shock value. It seemed to have the desired effect. Brand looked as if he wanted to take her by the shoulders and shake her until her teeth rattled.

Instead he marched to the other side of the kitchen and rammed his hand through his hair with enough force that if he did it a few more times he'd require a hair transplant. He turned, opened his mouth as though he wanted to say something, but quickly snapped it shut.

"She's perfect for you." Even as she spoke, Erin realized how true that was. It hurt to admit it, more than she dared concede. Almost from the beginning Brand had mentioned his two friends, Romano and Catherine, blending their names together as if the two were actually one. It was understandable. The three worked together. They were the very best of friends. Alex was married to Ginger, but that left Brand free for Catherine.

"Erin —"

"No," she interrupted. "I mean it. Catherine is the perfect woman for you. First of all, she's navy, and —"

"I don't happen to be in love with her," he barked. His long legs ate up the distance between them in three giant strides. "Hasn't the last week told you anything? The last week, nothing," he corrected sharply. "The last seven months!"

His anger did little to faze her. The more she dwelled on the subject of Brand and

Catherine, the more sense it made to her. In fact, she didn't know why it hadn't occurred to her much sooner. It wasn't until she'd met the other woman that Erin had recognized the truth.

"I'm serious, Brand."

"I'm not," he snapped. "I've never so much as kissed Catherine. It would be like dating my own sister. I'm sure she feels the same way."

"Wrong." Breaking out of his hold, she reached for the coffeepot. As if she hadn't a care in the world, Erin ran water and measured the grounds, hoping the activity would hide the pain that was crowding her heart. The thought of Brand loving another woman nearly crippled her emotionally, yet she pressed the subject, driven by some unknown force.

"All right," Brand conceded, slowly, thoughtfully. "Let's say you're right, and Catherine does hold some romantic feelings for me — although I want you to know right now I think that's crazy. But for the sake of argument I'll accept that premise. We've been working together for nearly three years —"

"Make that four," Erin interrupted, continuing to busy herself by clearing away what remained of the dinner dishes.

"Okay, four years." His gaze narrowed, but apparently he wasn't willing to argue over minute details. "If I haven't fallen for

Catherine in all that time, then what makes you assume I'd ever consider marrying her, especially now that I'm in love with you?"

"It's so obvious."

"What is?" he cried impatiently.

"That you and Catherine should be together. It all fits. I doubt you'd ever find anyone who suits you better." Gaining momentum, she continued, "It's true, you and I share a certain amount of physical attraction, but beyond that we seem to constantly be at odds."

Brand made the growling sound a second time, and then shocked her by stepping forward and gripping her hard by the shoulders. He squeezed so tightly that he half lifted her from the floor. "You know what you're doing, don't you?" he demanded.

She stared up at him mutely, stunned by this sudden show of force. It was so unlike Brand, which revealed how accomplished she was at getting a reaction from him.

"You're avoiding another confrontation," he told her, his voice firm and angry. "You don't want to leave Hawaii, or more appropriately, you don't want to leave me. Wonderful, because frankly, I don't want you to go, either. I love you. I have for so long I can't remember what it was like to not love you. I refuse to think of marrying anyone but you. To have you suggest I take Catherine as my wife makes damn little sense." His hold on her relaxed, and her feet were once again safely planted on the linoleum.

Erin lowered her gaze, realizing he was right but hating like hell to admit it. She was looking to avoid a showdown, and that was exactly what would have happened had their discussion followed the lead he'd taken. Admitting how badly she wanted to remain in the islands with him had left the door wide open for trouble. Brand wanted her to stay, too.

She remained stiff in his arms for a moment. Then a sigh raked her shoulders and she relaxed against him, wrapping her arms around his middle.

"You're right," she whispered. "I'm sorry . . . so sorry."

Brand froze briefly and muttered something under his breath that Erin couldn't detect. As though he couldn't bear the tension another moment, he buried his hands in her hair and drew her firmly into contact with his muscular, trim body. She tilted her head to smile up at him, and Brand took advantage of the movement by placing his mouth over hers.

His kiss revealed a storehouse of need. His tongue probed her mouth, and she opened to him as naturally as a castle gate opens to an arriving king. A wide host of familiar sensations warmed her, a heat so intense it frightened her. It had always been this way between them. He touched her, and it was like fire licking at dry kindling. Her response to Brand continued to amaze Erin. He'd kiss her, and the excitement seemed to explode throughout her body. In the beginning, his kisses had produced a warm sort of pleasure, but since their six-month separation, every time he held her in his arms her response was one of hungry need.

She nestled into his embrace the way a robin settles into her nest, spreading its wings, securing itself against the storm. It felt so incredibly good to have him hold her. Nothing she had ever known compared to the feelings of security he supplied.

She dragged in a deep breath, savoring the scent of warm musk that was uniquely his. Brand groaned and deepened the kiss, and Erin welcomed the intimacy of his tongue stroking hers. Unable to remain still, she started to move against him. Her nipples had hardened and were tingling, and the only way to relieve that shocking pleasure was to rotate the upper half of her body against him.

A low, rough sound rumbled through his throat as he gripped her by the hips and pressed her flush against him, adjusting her stance to graphically demonstrate his powerful need for her.

It felt familiar and so very good. Erin locked her arms around his neck and moved with him, her grinding hips contrasting the action of his own, enhancing the pleasure a hundredfold. Erin felt as though she were on fire, hot and aching, wanting everything at once.

"Oh, baby," he whispered in a voice that was guttural.

The noise from behind was as unexpected as it was unwelcome. Brand jerked his head back and ground his teeth in wretched frustration.

"Hello," Bobby greeted enthusiastically, closing the sliding glass door as he casually strolled into the kitchen. "Dad sent me in here to ask what was taking you two so long."

Brand's gaze narrowed menacingly. "Tell your dad . . ."

"We'll be right out," Erin completed for him.

"When are we going to have the ice cream?" the youngster wanted to know, walking over to the freezer, opening the door and staring inside. "It's time we had dessert, don't you think?"

Erin nodded. "If you want, I'll dish it up now and you can help me carry it out to everyone."

The boy eagerly nodded his head. Then, glancing at Brand, he seemed to change his mind. "Only don't let Uncle Brand help you. He might kiss you again and then you'd both forget."

"I won't let him kiss me," Erin promised.

"Wanna bet?" Brand teased under his breath.

Bobby studied the two of them quizzically. "Uncle Brand?"

"Yes, Bob."

"Are you going to marry Erin?"

"Ah . . ."

"I think you should, and so does my dad."

A moment of tense silence filled the room. Erin swallowed the lump that threatened to choke her. Her eyes were locked with Brand's, and she struggled to look away, but his gaze refused to release her.

"I . . . Let's get that ice cream," Erin suggested, hoping she sounded carefree and enthusiastic when she felt neither.

Erin's suitcases were packed and ready for her flight as she walked through Alex and Ginger's home one last time before Brand arrived to drive her to the airport. She'd woken that morning with a heavy feeling in her chest that had only grown worse as the day progressed. She dared not question its origin or what she needed to do to relieve it.

She knew the answer as clearly as if a doctor had given her a written diagnosis. Leaving Brand was far more difficult than she'd ever dreamed it would be.

He hadn't pressured her to marry him. Not once. In fact, she was the one who'd brought up the subject, when she'd suggested he con-

239

sider Catherine for his wife. That idea had all too quickly backfired in her face. And rightly so. She'd been an utter fool to suggest Brand romantically involve himself with another woman. Even now, just musing over the thought brought with it an instant flash of regret and pain.

Erin liked Catherine, enjoyed her company and wished her well, but when it came to Brand, Erin had discovered she was far more territorial than she ever realized. The awareness came as something of a shock.

Brand arrived and loaded Erin's suitcases into the trunk of his car. If he was unusually quiet on the drive to Honolulu International, she didn't notice, since she didn't seem to have much she wanted to say, either.

They sat next to each other in the crowded gate area, tightly holding hands while waiting for her flight number to be called. Erin's throat was so tight, she couldn't have carried on a conversation had the fate of world peace depended on it.

Each second that ticked away seemed to suck the energy right out of the room. Apparently no one else noticed except Brand.

When her flight was called, those gathered around her stood and reached for their personal items and brought out their tickets.

The first few rows had boarded when Brand stood. "You'll need to go on board now." He stated it matter-of-factly, as if her going was of little importance to him.

She nodded and reluctantly came to her feet.

"You'll call once you arrive back in Seattle?"

Once again she nodded.

Brand smoothed his hands over her shoulders, and his gaze just managed to avoid hers. "I'm pulling as many strings as I can to transfer to one of the bases in Washington state."

He hadn't mentioned that earlier, and Erin's hopes soared. If Brand lived on any of the navy bases near Seattle, even if it was one across Puget Sound, it would help ease the impossible situation between them. Then they would have the luxury of allowing their relationship to develop naturally without thousands of miles stretching between them like a giant, unyielding void.

"You didn't say anything about that earlier," she said, hating the way the eagerness crept into her voice. That he was prepared to leave the admiral's staff to be closer to her spoke volumes about his commitment to her.

"I didn't mention it before because it isn't the least bit probable."

"Oh." Her hope and excitement quickly diminished.

The final boarding call for her flight was announced. Erin glanced over her shoulder, wanting more than she'd ever wanted anything to remain with Brand. Yet she knew she had to leave.

"I don't suppose . . ." Brand began enthusiastically, then stopped abruptly.

"You don't suppose what?"

"Never mind."

"Never mind? Obviously you had something you wanted to say."

"That won't work, either."

"What won't work?" she demanded impatiently.

"Have you ever considered moving to Hawaii?" he asked, without revealing the least bit of emotion either way.

She was so stunned by the suggestion that it left her breathless. "Moving to Hawaii?" she gasped.

As crazy as it seemed, the first thought that filtered into her brain was that she'd be forced to sell her grand piano with the house, and frankly, not that many folks would be interested in something that large, especially when it dominated a good portion of the living room.

"Never mind," Brand said irritably. "I already said that wouldn't work."

She stared up at him, wondering why he was so quick to downplay his own suggestion until she realized how unfeasible the idea actually was. She had her job and her home and her sturdy, hard-to-move furniture. What about the roots she was so carefully planting in the Seattle area? Her friends? The Women in Transition classes she taught evenings?

"I can't move."

Brand frowned and nodded. "I know. It was a stupid idea. Forget I suggested it."

The way their courtship was progressing, she'd leave behind everything that was important to her for Brand and move to Hawaii just in time for him to be transferred to Alaska. Knowing the way the navy worked, she could count on something like that happening.

The attendant's voice announcing the last call for her flight was an intrusion Erin didn't want or need.

"Why didn't you say something sooner?" she demanded. At least they could have discussed it without the pressure of her being forced to board the plane. As it was, they'd sat, holding hands, for an hour without uttering more than a few words.

"I shouldn't have said anything now." His gaze gentled, and he brushed the tips of his fingers across her cheek, his touch light and unbelievably tender. His eyes momentarily left hers. "You have to go," he told her in a voice that was low and gravelly.

"Yes . . . I know." But now that the time had arrived, Erin wasn't sure she could turn and walk away from Brand and manage to keep her dignity intact. Oh, hell, she didn't know what she was going to do. He was everything she ever dreamed she'd find in a man, and, at the same moment, her greatest fear.

He hugged her all too briefly, then dropped his arms and stepped away from her. Wanting more than anything to wear a smile when she left him, she beamed him one broad enough to challenge Miss America. Then, with a dignified turn, she headed for the jetway.

"Erin." Her name was issued in a low growl. He was at her side so fast it made her dizzy. He hauled her into his arms and kissed her with a hunger that left her weak and clinging.

"I'm sorry," the flight attendant said, standing at the gate. "You'll have to board now. The flight's ready to depart."

"Go ahead," Brand whispered, stepping away from her.

"Oh, Brand." Erin hated the way her eyes filled with ready tears. Mascara running down her cheeks ruined the image she was working so hard to leave in his mind.

"Go back to Seattle," Brand said harshly, "go ahead and go, before I end up pleading with you to stay."

"Where have you been all weekend?" Aimee demanded, walking directly past Erin and into her living room, carting a large paper sack in one hand and a cigarette in the other. "I must have called twenty times."

"I took a ride up to Vancouver."

"All by yourself?" She sounded incredulous. "Good grief, you just got back from a week's vacation in Hawaii. Don't tell me you needed to get away." She whirled around her, searching for some unknown object. "Where do you keep your ashtrays?"

Erin followed her friend into the kitchen while Aimee searched through a row of four drawers. She dragged the first one open, briefly scanning the contents, only to slam it closed.

Removing a small glass ashtray from the cupboard, Erin held it out in the palm of her hand to her co-worker. "When did you start smoking?" She couldn't remember seeing Aimee with a cigarette before.

"I smoked years ago, when I was young and stupid. It's really a filthy habit. Trust me, whatever you do, don't start." Even as she was speaking, she opened her purse and brought out a pack. It was a brand designed especially for women, and the smokes were thin and long.

"Aimee!" Erin cried. "What's happened to you?"

As if she suddenly needed to talk, Aimee pulled out a chair and collapsed into it, automatically crossing her legs. Her foot started to swing like a precision timepiece, moving so fast she was creating a brisk breeze.

"I stopped off to show you my new outfit,"

Aimee announced. "I bought it to wear for the settlement hearing. If Steve's going to divorce me, I want to look my absolute best."

"In other words, you want him to regret it."

"Exactly." For the first time, a smile cracked the tight line of her mouth.

"Why don't you just come right out and tell him that?"

"You're joking!"

"I'm not," Erin assured her. She'd been away seven days, and upon her return she'd barely recognized her best friend. Aimee had lost a noticeable amount of weight and was so uptight she should be on tranquilizers. The fact she'd taken up smoking was a symptom of a much deeper problem.

"Steve and I are no longer on speaking terms."

"But I thought the two of you had never gotten along better."

"That was before," Aimee explained, grinding the cigarette butt in the ashtray.

"Before what?"

"Before . . . everything."

"Are you sure you're not misinterpreting the situation?" Erin didn't know Steve well, but she would have thought he was more fair-minded than that.

"That's not the half of it." The more Aimee talked, the faster her leg swung. Erin didn't dare focus her attention on the moving foot, lest it hypnotize her.

"You mean there's more?"

"Someone's moved into the duplex with him."

The pain was alive in Aimee's eyes. "A woman?" Erin asked softly.

"I . . . I don't know, but I imagine it must be. I know my husband — he enjoys regular bouts of sex."

"How'd you know someone moved in with him?" Erin couldn't help being curious. She strongly suspected that her friend was doing a bit of amateur detective work and coming up with all the wrong conclusions.

"I happened to be in the neighborhood and decided it wouldn't do any harm to drive by his place and see what Steve was up to. I'm glad I did, too, because there was a white convertible parked in his driveway." She blew a cloud of smoke at the ceiling, and when she set the cigarette down Erin noted that her hands were trembling.

"A white convertible?"

"Come on, Erin," Aimee said with a heavy note of sarcasm. "I'm not stupid. It was after midnight."

"That explains everything?"

"You and I both know a woman's more likely to drive a white car. Men like theirs black or red. The way I figure it, either Steve's got some cupcake shacked up with him or else he's having himself a little fun on the side. My guess is he's been into side dishes for a good long time."

"Aimee, that's ridiculous."

"Not according to my attorney."

"What makes him suggest anything like that? Honestly, I think this whole thing's gotten out of hand. Not so long ago you claimed Steve wasn't the type to mess around." The picture of the man who'd come to their table to correct a wrong impression the night they were in the Mexican restaurant played in Erin's mind.

"I called my lawyer first thing the following morning and gave him the license plate number. If Steve's fooling around, and I'm confident he is, then he's going to hear about it in court. If he wants another relationship, then the least he could do was wait for the ink to dry on the divorce decree."

Erin couldn't believe what she was hearing. Then again, it shouldn't shock her. Through the class she taught at the community college, she'd seen the emotional trauma, the bitterness and the pain of divorce cripple even the strongest women.

What surprised Erin was that this was Aimee. Calm, unruffled Aimee. In the time they'd worked together, Erin had seen her friend handle one explosive situation after another, competently, without accusation or blame.

"Anyway," Aimee said, reaching for the

Nordstrom bag at her side, "I wanted you to see the new dress I got for the court date. God knows I can't afford it, but I bought it anyway." She carefully unwrapped the tissue from around the silk blouse and skirt that was a bright shade of turquoise.

"Oh, Aimee, it's gorgeous."

"I thought so, too. I'll look stunning, won't I?"

Erin nodded. She wouldn't be able to go inside the judge's chambers with her friend. According to court rules, Erin would have to wait in the hallway, but then, all Aimee really needed was emotional support before and after.

"By the way, what were you doing in Canada this weekend?" Aimee asked, waving the cigarette smoke away from Erin's face. She glanced at the tip and extinguished it with a force that nearly pushed the ashtray from the table.

Erin hesitated, then decided that the truth was the best policy. "I needed to get away."

"I might remind you, you just spent the last week *away*."

"I know." In the five days since her return, Erin had spoken to Brand twice. Once, briefly, shortly after she'd arrived home. Then, later in the week, he'd contacted her again. He'd sounded tired and out of sorts. Although they'd spoken for several minutes, Erin had come away from the conversation feeling lonely and depressed.

As much as she tried to avoid doing so, Erin dwelt a good deal on what she'd suggested to Brand about him and Catherine. It hurt to think of Brand with another woman. *Hurt,* she decided, was too mild a word to describe the fiery pain that cut a wide path through her heart when she considered the situation. It would solve everything if the two of them were to fall in love. They had so much in common, including an appreciation of the many exciting aspects of navy life. Exciting to everyone, that is, who could accept the policies and the programs of a military lifestyle.

Someone who wasn't a navy brat. Someone who didn't know any better.

"Erin?" Aimee said softly. "Are you all right?"

"Oh, sure. I'm sorry," she said, forcefully bringing herself back to the present. "Were you saying something I missed?"

"No." But the other woman regarded her closely. "You never did tell me much about Hawaii. How was your time with Brand?"

"Wonderful." If anything, it had been too wonderful. She'd cherished each minute, greedy for time alone with him. They'd both been selfish, not wanting to share their precious days with others.

No one had seemed to mind. In fact, it had been as if Brand's friends were going out of their way to arrange it so.

"I hear Hawaii is really beautiful," Aimee continued. "At one time, Steve and I were planning a trip there for our tenth wedding anniversary."

"It is beautiful."

"But you wouldn't want to live there?"

The question took her by surprise. Erin blinked, not knowing how to answer. Could she live in Hawaii? Of course. The question didn't even need consideration. Anyone would enjoy paradise. If Brand were to own a business there, she'd marry him in a minute and plan on settling down and building an empire with him. But Brand was part of the military, and if she were to link her life with his, then she'd have to be willing to whole-heartedly embrace that lifestyle, and she didn't know if she could.

"Well?" Aimee pressed.

"No," Erin said automatically. "I don't think I could live in Hawaii."

"Me either," her friend muttered, and reached for a cigarette. "At least not now. Someplace cold and isolated interests me more at the minute."

"Greenland?"

"Greenland," Aimee echoed. "That would be perfect." She averted her eyes and pretended to remove a piece of lint from the leg of her slacks. "So," she said, expelling a breath sharply. "You'll meet me at the courthouse Monday morning?"

"I'll be there."

"Thanks. I knew I could count on you."

The phone rang just then, and Erin leaned toward the wall to reach for it.

"Hello," she said automatically.

There was no response for a couple of seconds, long enough for Erin to believe it was a crank call.

"Erin MacNamera?" Her name sounded as though it came from a long way off, but not long-distance. The telltale hum was decidedly missing.

"Yes, this is Erin MacNamera." The female voice was vaguely familiar, but Erin couldn't place it.

"This is Marilyn . . . from class. I'm really sorry to trouble you," she said, clearly trying to disguise the fact that she was weeping.

"It's no trouble, Marilyn. It's good to hear from you. How are you? I haven't talked to you in weeks."

"I'm fine." She paused and then gave a short, abrupt laugh. "No, I'm not . . . all right. In fact, I thought I should call someone. Do you have time to talk right now?"

Chapter Twelve

That night, after Aimee's settlement hearing, Erin woke from a sound sleep with tears in her eyes. She lay for several moments, trying to remember what she'd been dreaming that had been so bitterly sad. Whatever it was had escaped her. She rolled over and glanced at her clock, then sighed. It would be several hours yet before the alarm sounded.

Snuggling up with her pillow, she intended to go back to sleep, and was somewhat surprised to discover she couldn't. The tears returned, rolling down her cheek at an alarming pace.

Sitting up, she reached for a tissue, blowing her nose hard. She couldn't understand what was happening to her or why she would find it so necessary to weep. A parade of possible reasons marched through her mind. Hormones. She was missing Brand. Her experience with Aimee that morning. Marilyn. There were any number of excuses why she would wake up weeping. But none that she could readily understand.

She drew the covers over her shoulders and lay staring into space. How she wished Brand were with her then. He'd take her in his arms and comfort her in a soft and reassuring way. He'd kiss away her doubts and her fears. Then he'd touch her in all the ways he knew would please her and gently coax the tears away with his warmth and his wit.

Erin missed him more in that moment than she had in the six months he'd been away at sea.

She closed her eyes, and faces and tension crowded her mind. They were the faces of the men and women she'd seen in court that morning. The eerie silence that had nearly stifled her as she'd waited for Aimee and Steve to come out of the judge's chambers.

The silence had been like nothing she'd ever experienced. Long rows of mahogany benches had lined the hallway. It was ironic that they should resemble church pews. Lawyers conferred with their clients while waiting their turn with the judge. Aimee must have crossed and uncrossed her legs a hundred times, she'd been so nervous. Then she'd started swinging her foot fast enough to cause a draft.

Later, when she and Steve had gone before the judge, Erin had been surrounded by the silence. The wounded, eerie silence of pain.

Erin was worried about Marilyn, too. The older woman had phoned needing to talk. The pain and the anger of her circumstances had gotten so oppressive she couldn't tolerate it another minute. Reaching out for help was something they'd discussed in class. Erin had spent almost an hour on the phone with Marilyn, listening while she talked out her pain.

Marilyn was just beginning to draw upon that well of inner strength. Erin had every confidence that the older woman would come away strong and secure. She wasn't so sure about the young woman she'd seen in the courthouse earlier that day, however.

The desperate look on the woman's face returned to haunt her now. She'd been weeping softly and trying to disguise her tears. Trembling. Shaken. She looked as if she'd been knocked off balance.

Erin's heart throbbed anew at the anguish she'd viewed in the young mother's eyes. She knew nothing of her circumstances, only what she'd overheard while waiting for Aimee. Yet the woman's red eyes and haunting look returned to torment Erin hours later.

After the hearing before the judge, Aimee had been shaken to the core, and Erin had suggested they go out for lunch instead of rushing back to the office. Aimee hadn't said much, and the two had eaten in silence. It was the same throbbing silence Erin had experienced earlier in the courtroom.

Now, hours later, in the wee hours of the morning, it was back again, nearly suffocating her with its intensity, and she hadn't a clue why.

Sitting at his desk, Brand had a vague uneasy feeling he couldn't quite place. He'd heard regularly from Erin since her return to the mainland.

When it came to dealing with his sweet Irish rose, he was playing his hand close to his chest. Being patient and not pressing her for a commitment was damned difficult.

He loved her, there was no question in his mind about that. He also knew it was asking a good deal of her to love him back. It would be a whole lot easier if he wasn't navy. Erin wanted stability, permanence, roots. All Brand had to do was prove to her she could have all that and still be his wife. The military had provided more security than he'd ever known as a civilian.

The navy was his life, and Brand believed that, in time, Erin would come around to his way of thinking. She loved him. A smile courted the edges of his mouth as he recalled their time together in the surf and Erin's eager response to his touch. They'd never come closer to making love than they had that night. It was something of a miracle that they hadn't.

When they'd first met and dated, the physical attraction between them had been nearly overpowering. He'd never experienced anything like it. If they were together for any length of time, he could be assured that the magnetism between them would reach explosive levels. That hadn't changed, but another dimension had been added in the months they'd known each other. They'd bonded emotionally. Erin had become a large part of Brand's life. She'd helped define who he was, how he thought and the way he governed his actions. She was the first person he thought of when he rolled out of bed in the morning. Generally, he woke regretting that she wasn't at his side, and mused how long it would take for her to come to her senses and marry him.

Thoughts of her followed him through most of the day. He lived for the mail. If there was a letter from her, he read it two and three times straight through, savoring each word. Often right then and there, with his concerns fresh in his mind, he sat down and wrote her back. Brand had never been much of a writer. Letters were time-consuming, and he sometimes had trouble expressing himself with the written word. Not wanting to be misinterpreted, he'd opt for a quick phone call instead. Sea duty this last time around had been a challenge for him in more ways than one, but he'd learned some valuable lessons. He needed to hear from Erin.

Not wanted. Needed.

While on duty aboard the *Blue Ridge*, he'd been forced to admit for the first time how much he did need her. He'd tried not to love her, he'd attempted to put her out of his mind and his life, but he'd discovered to his chagrin that he was unable to do so.

Erin MacNamera was the most important person in his world. Since he couldn't give her up, he had no other option but to be patient and bide his time.

The vague uneasy feeling persisted most of the afternoon.

Catherine's news was equally unsettling.

"What do you mean you're being transferred to Bangor?" Brand demanded. He didn't use profanity often, but he couldn't hold back a couple of choice words when he learned Catherine was being stationed in Washington state.

"Hey," she argued, "I didn't ask for this. Personally, I'm not all that thrilled about it."

"You didn't ask for it, I *did*." Brand would have been willing to surrender his commission for the opportunity to move closer to Erin. It seemed he was thwarted at every turn when it came to loving her.

A letter from Erin was waiting for him when he arrived home that evening. He stared at the envelope, grateful that something good had come of this day. He'd been beginning to have his doubts.

Standing in the middle of his compact living room, he tore open the letter with his index finger and read:

Dearest Brand,

This is the most difficult letter I've ever written in my life. I've started it so many times, tried to make sense of my feelings, praying all the while that you'll understand and forgive me.

I woke up early the other morning, weeping. Aimee had needed me to go to the courthouse with her for her settlement hearing. I had waited outside in the hallway for her, and while I was there I saw a woman in her early twenties crying. Never have I had any experience affect me more profoundly. There was so much pain in that hallway. It seemed to reach out and grab hold of me. Perhaps it was because Aimee's settlement hearing followed on the heels of an episode with Margo. She's had her ups and downs over the last nine months, small triumphs followed by minor setbacks. I've worked with so many divorcing women since I started my job. I'm beginning to wonder if anyone stays married anymore. How can Margo's husband walk away after thirty years of marriage? How could he possibly abandon her now? It doesn't make sense to me.

Even Aimee surprises me. I knew she and Steve were having problems, but I never dreamed matters would go this far.

I suppose you're wondering what Aimee's settlement hearing and Margo's problems have to do with the fact I woke up crying. Trust me, it took a long time for me to make the connection myself.

Deep down, in the innermost part of my being, the trauma involving Aimee and Margo forced me to face up to my true feelings regarding our relationship. I do love you, Brand. So much so that it sometimes frightens me, but we can't continue, we can't go on pretending our differences are all going to magically disappear someday. Falling in love caught us both unaware. You certainly didn't intend to leave Seattle caring about me, and I never intended to love you. It happened, and we both let it. Now we're left to deal with the way we've tangled our two lives.

I realize my thoughts are all so scrambled yet, and you don't have a clue of what I'm trying to say. I'm not even sure I can explain it myself. I suppose I recognized it first when I talked to Margo late one evening when she was suffering from a bout of deep emotional pain. Following on the heels of that was Aimee's settlement hearing.

I know you're hoping we'll soon be married. You've been so patient and understanding. I knew how much you truly loved me when you stopped pressuring me to become your wife.

In the last few weeks, I've given a good

deal of thought to your proposal, and to be honest was leaning in that direction.

I've made my decision, and it was the most heart-wrenching one of my life. I can't marry you, Brand. It came to me recently why. It isn't because I don't love you enough. Please believe that. Learning not to love you will likely take me a lifetime.

If we do marry, someday down the road we're going to divorce. Our differences are fundamental ones. You're a part of the navy. I honestly believe that what attracted me to you so strongly was your likeness to my father. You certainly don't resemble him physically, but on the inside you two could be mistaken for blood relatives. You think so much alike. Your lives don't belong to yourselves, or your family. They belong to good ol' Uncle Sam.

I had eighteen years of that, and I can't and won't accept that crazy lifestyle a second time. I hated it then, and I'll hate it now.

This isn't a new issue. It's the same one we've been pounding out almost from the moment we met. The problem is, I grew to love you so much I was willing to give in on this, thinking that if we married everything would work out all right. I was burying my head in the sand and pretending. But someday in the future, we'd both have paid dearly for my refusal to accept the truth. By then there'd probably be children, too. I couldn't bear for our children to suffer through a divorce.

It's ironic that I work almost exclusively with divorced women. Month after month, class after class, and it still didn't hit me how ugly and painful it is to dissolve a marriage until I saw what's happened to Aimee. She and Steve are in so much pain. It hurts me to see her suffer. I barely know Steve, and I hurt for him, too. My attitude toward marriage has gotten so sarcastic lately. I'm beginning to question if anyone should willingly commit their lives to another.

Aimee's so bitter now. I think she's convinced herself she hates Steve. The woman in the hallway at the courthouse, too. I felt something so strongly when I saw her. That sounds crazy, doesn't it? Everyone there was in such deep emotional pain. When I thought about it, I realized that so many of those men and women started out just the way we are. At one time they'd been as deeply in love as we are now. Only we'd be starting off with a mark against us, feeling the way I do about the navy.

Please accept my decision, Brand. Don't write me back. Don't call me. Please let this be the end.

It's been the most painful and difficult decision of my life. Yet deep in my heart I know it's the right one. You may disagree with me now, but someday, when you look back over this time, I believe you'll realize I'm doing the right thing for us both, although God help me, it's the most painful decision I've ever made.

Thank you for loving me. Thank you for teaching me about myself. And please, oh, please, be happy.

Erin

Brand closed his eyes. He felt as though a two-by-four had been slammed into his stomach. For one frenzied moment he thought he might be sick. It was the oddest sensation, as though he'd been physically attacked, badly injured, and was experiencing the first stages of shock.

It took him a couple of minutes to compose himself. His heart was pounding inside his chest like a huge Chinese gong. He paced back and forth in fruitless frustration, sorting through his limited options.

Before he leaped to conclusions, he needed to reread Erin's letter and determine how serious she actually was. He did so, sitting himself down at his desk and digested each word, seeking . . . hell, he didn't know what he was looking for. Loopholes? An indication, any evidence he might find, that she didn't mean what she wrote. A glimmer of hope.

The second reading, and later a third, told him otherwise. Erin meant every single word. She wanted out of the relationship, and for both their sakes, she didn't want to hear from him again.

A week had passed since Erin had mailed Brand the final letter.

"Coward," she muttered under her breath. This was what she got for not confronting him over the phone. She'd known from the first that she was taking the easy way out. Originally she'd told herself she was looking to avoid any arguments or lengthy discussions. Only later was she willing to admit that she was a wimp.

"Are you back to talking to yourself again?" Aimee muttered from her desk across the aisle from Erin's.

"What did I say this time?"

"Something about being a coward."

"Oh . . . I guess maybe I did." It was funny, really. Ironic, too, that she'd made the most courageous, and by far the most difficult, decision of her life, and a week later she was calling herself a coward.

"I would do the same thing all over again," she whispered, and her voice caught slightly. Caught on the pain. Caught on the regret.

"Are you still carrying on about Brand?" Aimee demanded unsympathetically.

Erin nodded.

"Trust me, all of womankind is better off without men. They use and abuse, in that order," Aimee said, and snickered softly. "I'm beginning to sound a bit jaded, aren't I? Sorry about that. You've been in the dumps all week, and I haven't been much help."

"Don't worry about it. You're having problems of your own."

"Not so much anymore. Steve and I have come to terms. The final papers are being drawn up, and the whole messy affair is going to be over. At last. I didn't think this was ever going to end."

"Are you doing anything after work?" Going home to an empty, dark house, even with a grand piano to greet her, had long since lost its appeal. Before she'd written the final letter to Brand, she'd hurried home, praying there'd be a letter waiting there for her. But there wouldn't be any more letters. At least not from Brand. Once she realized that, she'd suddenly started looking for excuses not to go home after work.

"What do you have in mind?" Aimee asked.

"James Bradshaw, the famous divorce attorney, is giving a workshop on prenuptial agreements. I recommended it to the women in my class. I thought you might like to join us."

"Hey, sorry, I can't do anything tonight,"

Aimee answered in a preoccupied voice. She shuffled a couple of files before she continued. "Prenuptial agreement? Good grief, Erin, you're not even married and you're planning for a divorce."

"Not me," Erin replied. "It's for the women in my class. After seeing what's happened to Marilyn and women like her, and now you, I think it's smart to have everything down in black and white."

Aimee busied herself at her desk. "Personally, I don't think it's a good idea to start out a marriage by planning for a divorce."

Erin stared at her friend, not knowing what to think. Aimee was at the tail end of a divorce that had cut her to the quick. If anyone understood the advisability of prenuptial agreements, Erin thought, it should be her friend.

"Listen —" Aimee rolled back her chair and sighed. "Forget I said that. I'm the last person in the world who should be giving romantic advice. My marriage is in shambles and . . . I feel like one of the walking wounded myself. Maybe the lecture isn't such a bad idea after all."

"Go on," Erin urged. "I'd be interested in hearing your opinion."

Aimee didn't look as if she trusted her own thoughts. "As I said, I don't think it's a good idea to start off a marriage by planning for divorce. I know that's an unpopular point of view, especially in this day and age, but it just doesn't feel right to me."

"How can you say that?" Erin cried. "You're going through a divorce yourself. Good grief, you've been through hell the last few months, and now all of a sudden you're making marriage sound like this glorious, wonderful state of being. As I recall, you and Steve can't carry on a civil conversation. What's changed?"

"A lot," Aimee announced solemnly. "And you, my friend, have the opportunity to gain from my experience."

Feeling uncomfortable, Erin looked away.

"We're both here day in and day out, working with women who are making new lives for themselves," Aimee continued. "But finding them a decent job is only the beginning. They've been traumatized, abandoned and left to deal with life on their own. If you want the truth, I'm beginning to believe our thinking's becoming jaded. Not everyone ends up divorced. Not everyone will have to go through what these women have. It's just that we deal with it each and every day until our own perception of married life has been warped."

"But you and Steve —"

"I know," Aimee argued. "Trust me, I know. I pray every day I'm doing the right thing by divorcing Steve."

Erin was praying the same thing herself for

the both of them. "But if you're having second thoughts, shouldn't you be doing something?"

"Like what?" Aimee suggested, her voice flippant. "Steve's already involved with another woman."

"You don't know that."

"Deep down I do. You saw him the day we went to court. He wore that stupid green tie just to irritate me, and the looks he gave me . . . I can't begin to describe to you the way he glanced at me, as if . . . as if he couldn't believe he'd ever been married to me in the first place. He couldn't wait for the divorce to be final."

"But I thought this was a friendly divorce."

Aimee's gaze fell to her hands. "There's no such thing as a friendly divorce. It's too damn painful for everyone involved."

"Oh, Aimee, I feel so bad for you and Steve."

"Why should you?" she asked, the sarcastic edge back in her voice. "We're both getting exactly what we want."

Erin knew nothing more that she could say. She didn't have any excuse to linger around the office. The lecture wasn't until seven, and it was optional as far as her class was concerned. She didn't have to be there herself, but she thought it would help kill time, which was something that was weighing heavily on her these days.

Erin's thoughts were heavy as she walked outside the double glass doors of the fifteen-story office complex. The wind had picked up and was biting-cold. She hunched her shoulders and tucked her hands inside her coat pockets as she headed for the parking lot on Yesler.

With her head down, it was little wonder she didn't notice the tall, dark figure standing next to her car. It wasn't until she was directly in front of him that she realized someone was blocking her path.

When she looked up, her heart, in a frenzy, flew into her throat.

Brand stood there, his eyes as cold and biting as the north wind.

"Brand," she whispered, hardly able to speak, "what are you doing here?"

"You didn't want me to write you or contact you by phone. But you didn't say anything about not seeing you in person. If you want to break everything off, fine, I can accept that. Only you're going to have to do it to my face."

Chapter Thirteen

"You couldn't let it go, could you?" Erin cried, battling with an anger that threatened to consume her. Tears blurred Brand's image before her, and for a second she couldn't make out his features. When she did, her heart ached at the sight of him.

"No, I couldn't leave it," Brand returned harshly. "You want to end it, then fine, have it your way. But I'm not going to make it easy for you."

"Oh, Brand," she whispered, her anger vanishing as quickly as it had come, "do you honestly believe it was easy?"

"Say it, Erin. Tell me you want me out of your life."

He towered over her like a thundercloud, dark and menacing. Erin's feet felt as if they were planted ankle-deep in concrete. She needed to put a few inches of distance between them, grant them both necessary breathing room. As it was, she was having a difficult time getting oxygen into her lungs.

"Could we go someplace else and discuss this?" She barely managed the tightly worded request. The urge to break down was nearly overwhelming. It hurt as much to talk as to breathe.

Of his own accord, Brand stepped away from her. "Where?"

"There's an . . . Italian restaurant not far from here." The suggestion came off the top of her head, and the minute she said it, Erin realized attempting to talk would be impossible there.

"I'm not discussing this with a roomful of people listening in on the conversation."

"All right, you choose." A restaurant hadn't been a brilliant idea, but Erin couldn't think of anyplace else they could go.

She wished with everything in her heart that Brand had accepted her letter and left it at that. Having him confront her unexpectedly like this made everything so much more difficult.

"If we're going to talk, it has to be someplace private," he insisted.

"Ah . . ." Erin hesitated.

"My hotel room," Brand suggested next, but he said it as though he expected her to argue with him.

"Okay," she agreed, not questioning the wisdom of his idea. Her primary thought was to get this over with as quickly as possible. It didn't matter where they spoke, because in her heart she knew it wouldn't take more than a few minutes. "I don't have a lot of time."

"You've got a date?" He bit out the question.

"No . . . I'm suppose to be at a lecture."

"When?"

"By seven."

"You'll be there." Brand took off walking, expecting her to follow behind. She did so reluctantly, wishing she could avoid this confrontation and knowing she couldn't.

His pace was brisk, and Erin practically had to trot in order to keep up with his long-legged strides. They'd gone four or five blocks when he entered the revolving glass door that led to the tastefully decorated hotel lobby.

He paused outside the elevator for Erin to catch up to him. She was breathless by the time she traipsed across the plush red-and-white carpet.

In all the time she'd known Brand, she'd never seen him quite like this. He was so unemotional, so unfeeling. Aloof, as if nothing she could say or do would disconcert him.

His room was on the tenth floor. He unlocked and held open the door for her, and she walked inside. It was a standard room with a double bed, a nightstand and a dresser. In the corner, next to the window were a table and two olive-green upholstered chairs.

"Go ahead and sit down," he instructed brusquely. "I'll have room service send up some coffee."

Erin nodded, walked across the room and

settled in the crescent-shaped chair.

Brand picked up the phone, pushed a button and requested the coffee. When he'd finished, he surprised her by sauntering to the other side of the compact room and sitting on the edge of the mattress.

Erin's gaze fell to her hands. "I wish it didn't have to be this way. I'm so sorry, Brand," she said in a small voice.

"I didn't come all this way for an apology."

He seemed to be waiting for something more, but Erin didn't know what it was, and even if she had, she wasn't sure she could have supplied it. The strained silence was so loud, it was all Erin could do not to press her hands over her ears.

"Say something," she pleaded. "Don't just sit there looking so angry you could bite my head off."

"I'm not angry," he corrected, clenching his fists, "I'm downright furious." He bounded to his feet and stalked across the compact room. "A letter," he said bitingly, and turned to glare down at her. "You didn't have the decency to talk this out with me. Instead, you did it in a letter."

"I . . . was afraid . . ."

She wasn't allowed to finish. Brand advanced two steps toward her, then stopped. "Have I ever given you a reason to fear me? Ever? Am I so damn difficult to talk to? Is that it?"

"I wasn't afraid of you."

"A letter doesn't make a whole lot of sense."

"I know," she whispered woefully. "It seemed the best way at the time. I didn't mean to hurt you. Trust me, it hasn't exactly been a piece of cake for me, either."

"Explain it to me, Erin, because I'm telling you right now, I can't make heads or tails out of that letter. You love me, but you can't marry me because you're afraid we'll end up divorcing someday and you don't want to put our children through the trauma. Do you realize how crazy that sounds?"

"It isn't crazy," she cried, vaulting to her feet. "Okay, so maybe I didn't explain myself very well, but you weren't there. You don't know."

"I wasn't where?"

"In the courthouse that day with Aimee." She covered her face with her hands and shook her head, trying to dispel the ready images that popped into her head. The same ones that had returned to haunt her so often. The young mother, who was consulting with her attorney and trying so hard to disguise the fact that she was crying. Aimee, her legs swinging like a pendulum gone berserk while she smoked like a chimney the whole time, pretending she was as cool as a milkshake. The heartache. The pain that was all so tangible. And the silence. That horrible, wounded silence.

"What makes you so certain we'll divorce?" Brand demanded.

Lowering her hands, she sadly shook her head. "Because you're navy."

"I'm getting damn tired of that argument."

"That's because you've ignored my feelings about the military from the first. I told you the night we met how I felt about dating anyone in the military. I warned you . . . but you insisted. You refused to leave well enough alone —"

"Come on, Erin," he argued bitterly, "I didn't exactly kidnap you and force you to date me. You were as eager to get to know me as I was you."

"But I —"

"You don't have a single quarrel. You wanted this. You can argue until you're blue in the face, but it won't make a damn bit of difference."

"I can't marry you."

"Fine, then we'll be lovers." He jerked off his blue uniform jacket and started on the buttons of his military-issue shirt.

Stunned, Erin didn't move. She couldn't believe what she was seeing. "I . . . I . . . what about the coffee?"

"Right. I'll cancel it." He walked over to the phone and dialed room service. When he turned back to her, he seemed surprised that she was still wearing her coat. "Go on," he urged. "Get undressed."

Erin's mind raced for an excuse. "You're not serious," she said, crowding the words together.

"The hell I'm not. I don't suppose you're protected," he said, pausing momentarily. "Well, don't worry about it. I'll take care of it." He sat on the end of the bed and removed his shoes, then stood and methodically undid his belt. While she stood stunned, barely able to believe what she was viewing, he unzipped his pants and calmly stepped out of them.

Erin sucked in a sharp breath and backed up two or three paces. Brand must have sensed her movement, because he glanced up, seemingly surprised to find her standing so far away from him.

"Take off your clothes," he ordered. He stood before her in his boxer shorts and T-shirt, seemingly impatient for her to remove her own things.

"Brand, I . . . can't do this."

"Why not?" he demanded. "You were plenty eager before. As I recall, you once told me you'd rather we were lovers. I was the one fool enough to insist we marry."

"Not like this," she pleaded. "Not when you're so . . . cold."

"Trust me, Erin, a few kisses will warm us both right up." He walked over to her and systematically unbuttoned her coat. She stood, numb with disbelief. This couldn't actually be happening, could it? In answer to her silent question, her coat fell to the floor.

Brand's eyes were on hers, and she noted that the anger was gone, replaced with some emotion she couldn't name. With his gaze continuing to hold hers, Brand reached behind her for the zipper at the back of her dress. The hissing sound of it gliding open filled the room as though a swarm of bees were directly behind them. She raised her hands in a weak protest, but Brand ignored her.

Easing the material over her smooth shoulders, he paused midway in his journey to press his moist, hot mouth to the hollow of her throat. Tense and frightened, Erin jerked slightly, then reached out and gripped the edge of the table to steady herself.

"Brand," she pleaded once more. "Please don't . . . not like this."

"You'll be saying a lot more than please before we're finished," he assured her.

His mouth traveled at a leisurely pace up the side of her neck, across the sensitized skin at the underside of her jaw. Despite everything, his nearness warmed her blood.

Everything was different now. He was loving and gentle and so incredibly male. He smelled of musk. Erin had forgotten how much she enjoyed the manly fragrance that was Brand. He turned his head and nuzzled her ear with his nose, and unable to resist him any longer, Erin slipped her arms around his middle and tentatively held on to his waist.

He rewarded her with a soft kiss and braced his feet slightly apart. Then, dragging her by the hips, he urged her forward until she was tucked snugly between his parted thighs. Once she was secure, he slipped her arms free of the restricting material of her dress and slowly eased it over her hips.

Erin wasn't ready for this new intimacy and resisted. Brand reacted by kissing her several times until she willingly parted her mouth to eagerly receive his kisses. The gathered silk material of her dress pooled at her feet.

His hands were at the waistband of her tap pants when he paused as though he expected her to resist him anew. "I think we should stop now," she whispered, knowing that if the loving continued much longer they'd both be lost.

"That's the problem," he whispered, his mouth scant inches from her own. "We both think too much. This time we're going to feel."

"Oh, Brand . . ." She was confused and uncertain but too needy to care.

"I want you, Erin, and by heaven, I fully intend to have you."

If she pushed him away or made the slightest protest, Erin was convinced, Brand would immediately cease their lovemaking. But she seemed incapable of doing either. All she could seem to manage was a weak mewling sound deep in her throat that encouraged Brand to take further liberties with her. She felt torn between the dictates of her body and the decree of her pride. She couldn't allow this to happen, and yet she was powerless to stop him.

He kissed her again and again. A trembling started in her knees, spreading to her thighs until she could barely support herself. She sagged against Brand. He accepted her weight, and without her quite figuring out how he managed it, Erin found herself sprawled across the mattress with Brand lying alongside her.

"My sweet Erin, oh, my love," he whispered, his eyes tender. "Tell me you want me. I need you to say it . . . just this once. Give me that to remember you by." The words were issued in sweet challenge between wild, carnal kisses.

"Oh, Brand." She breathed his name when she could, but talking, indeed breathing, had become less and less important.

"Say it," he demanded again, easing his hands over her flat, smooth stomach to caress the womanly part of her.

"Do you want me?" he whispered.

"Yes . . . oh, yes."

Erin had never felt as she did at that moment. Never so needy or so feminine. He kissed her and moved over her, his hands in her hair, lifting her mouth upward to meet his. Brand made her feel as if she were exploding from the inside out. This feeling, so beautiful, so brilliant and warm, filled her eyes with tears that splashed onto her cheeks.

He straddled her, eager now, his hands gripping the waistband of her tap pants. He paused when he noticed her tears.

Slowly he eased himself off her and sat on the edge of the mattress, his eyes closed. "I can't do it. Dear God in heaven, I can't do it."

Erin couldn't move. Her breasts were heaving, and tears rained down the side of her face and leaked onto the bedspread. "It would never work between us, Brand. I couldn't bear to go through a divorce." She paused and twisted her head away so that she wouldn't have to look at him.

"You honestly believe that, don't you?" He slowly shook his head.

"I do mean it. Would I put us through this torture if I didn't?"

"Honest to God, I don't know." Before she fully realized his intention, Brand moved off the bed and reached for his clothes.

Erin sat up, distributing her weight on the palms of her hands. He was actually dressing. A few moments earlier he'd been preparing to make love to her, and now he was dressing. "I want you, Erin," he said when he'd finished. "I'll probably regret not making love to you to the day they lower me into my grave."

"But why . . . aren't you?"

"Damned if I know. Maybe it's because I count your father as a friend." He paused and rubbed his hand across his face. "More likely I'm afraid if we make love, once would never be enough, and we'd spend the rest of our lives the way we have the last eight months. Personally, I can't deal with that. I don't think you could, either."

He was right; she'd never been so miserable.

"Go ahead and get dressed."

"First you demand that I undress, now you want me to dress. I wish you'd kindly make up your mind," she muttered peevishly. She scooted off the mattress and reached for her clothes, jerking them on impatiently.

"You claimed you wanted to talk," she reminded him once she'd finished.

He nodded. "Coming here wasn't a brilliant idea." His smile was decidedly off center. He hesitated, his eyes sad. "My anger frightened you?"

"Only at first, when you seemed so indifferent."

He nodded and leaned against the wall, as if standing upright were becoming too much of a burden for him. "You meant what you said in that letter?"

Erin closed her eyes and nodded.

"I was afraid of that."

"Brand, I'd give anything if I could be different. Anything, but —"

"Don't," he said, cutting her off. "It isn't necessary."

"Please try to understand," she pleaded softly. "I went through hell. For nights on end I'd wake up weeping and not know why, and then I realized it all boiled down to what was happening to you and me. Deep down I knew it would be that way."

Brand said nothing. She'd pleaded with him not to argue with her, begged him to accept the inevitable, but his silence now was like having a knife plunged directly into her soul.

"There isn't anything more to say then, is there?" he said, his back as stiff as a flagpole as he walked over to the closet and removed his suitcase.

"You're leaving?" It wasn't her most brilliant deduction in the past year.

"There isn't any reason to stay."

No, she admitted miserably to herself. There wasn't. Reluctantly, she stood, her heart aching as it never had. Before she left him, before she walked out of his life, she had to say one last thing. When she spoke, her voice wavered slightly, then leveled out. "You probably hate me now. . . . I wouldn't blame you if you did. But please, in the future, when you can, try to think kindly of me. Please know that more than anything I want you to be happy."

"I will be happy," he said forcefully. "Damn happy."

She nodded, although she didn't believe it would be true for a good long while for either of them.

"Go ahead and marry your stockbroker, or attorney, or whoever it is who interests you," he continued. "Settle down in your four-bedroom colonial with your two point five children and live the good life." Brand's words were biting and sharp. Forcefully he shoved his clothes inside the suitcase, not taking the time to fold them properly. "Plant those roots so deep they'll reach all the way to China."

Erin blinked back tears. He was so bitter, and there was nothing she could say to make it better. She stiffened, knowing he needed to vent his frustration and his pain.

"By all means, marry your stockbroker," he repeated forcefully. "Security is everything. Tell yourself that often, because I have the feeling you're going to need to remember it."

Erin knotted her fists at her side. The lump in her throat had grown to gargantuan proportions.

"Goodbye, Erin," he whispered as he eased the lid of the suitcase closed. He looked toward the door, silently asking that she walk out of his room as willingly as she was walking out of his life.

"I know it hurts, but it's better this way," she whispered, her voice low and choppy.

He paused and grudgingly smiled at her. "Far better," he agreed.

Chapter Fourteen

"Come on, Erin," Aimee urged. "It's December. Liven up a little, would you?"

"I'm alive." Which was stretching the truth. Oh, she functioned day to day and had for the past several weeks, since she'd last seen Brand. The emotional pain had been intolerable in the beginning, but, as expected, the intensity had lessened. She'd counted on being much better by now, however.

Severing the relationship with Brand was what she wanted, she reminded herself. Marrying Brand would have been the biggest mistake of her life. It was amazing how many times a day she was forced to remind herself of that.

"How about doing some Christmas shopping after work?" Aimee suggested.

"Thanks anyway, but I finished mine last week." Erin appreciated the offer, but try as she would, she couldn't muster much enthusiasm for the holidays. The crowds irritated her, and she hated being impatient and grumpy when everyone around her was filled with good cheer.

Bah, humbug! Erin had always loved the holidays.

As hard as she tried not to, she couldn't

help wondering about Brand. Was he still in Hawaii? Had he started dating? Was he happy?

By force of will, Erin managed to avoid thoughts of him during the day. Every time her mind turned to the Hawaii-based lieutenant, she immediately focused on another subject. World peace. Jalapeño jelly. Scissors. Anything and everything but Brand.

It was later, when she was about to slip into the welcome void of sleep, that she found herself most vulnerable. She'd be wandering between the two worlds when Brand would casually stroll into her mind.

He didn't speak; not once had he uttered a word. He just stood there, straight and tall, dressed in his uniform. Proud. Strong. Earnest.

Erin tried to make his image disappear. More than once she'd sat bolt upright in bed and demanded that he clear out of her mind. He always did, without question, but when she lay back down, she always regretted that he was gone.

There had been one improvement, if she could call it that. The episodes when she woke in the middle of the night weeping for no apparent reason had passed. But it was damn little comfort for all the lonely days and nights those unexplained bouts had spawned.

Erin and Aimee walked out of the office

together. The air was filled with a joyous holiday flavor. Bells chimed at every street corner. Storefronts were decorated with large swags of evergreen draped above doorways, stretching from one business to the other. Huge red plastic bells adorned streetlights. Erin walked past it all, barely noticing.

"Call me if you change your mind," Aimee said before heading in the opposite direction.

"I will, thanks." But Erin already had her plans for the evening. She was going home, cuddling up in front of the television and mindlessly viewing situation comedies until it was bedtime. It wasn't exciting, nor was it inspiring, but a quiet dinner and television were the only things she could effectively deal with that night. After months of teaching sessions on self-acceptance and being kind to oneself, Erin was determined to follow her own advice.

Erin's mail contained three Christmas cards. The first was from Terry, an old college friend. Terry had married the previous year, and her printed Christmas letter shared the happy news of her pregnancy.

"Terry with a baby," Erin mused aloud, remembering distinctly how they'd both been certain they were destined to remain single the rest of their natural lives.

The second card was from Marilyn. Erin read her brief note with interest. The older woman was forming friendships and had attended a dance with a woman friend who had been widowed several years earlier. Marilyn's note ended with the happy news that she'd danced three times. She claimed she felt more like a wallflower than like Cinderella, but she was ready to attend another dance the following week.

The third Christmas card was from her parents. Erin read over the greeting and was pleased to note that her father had included a short typed sheet along with her mother's much thicker letter. She read her father's letter first.

Dear Erin,

Happy holidays. Your mother and I mailed off a package to you this afternoon, which should arrive in plenty of time for Christmas. I wish we could be together, but that's what happens when kids grow up and leave home. Your mother and I are going to miss being with you this year.

I don't have much news. Your mother will tell you everything that's up with your brother and sister. They're well and happy, and that's all that counts.

Now what's this I hear about you putting your house up for sale? I remember when you bought it you claimed you were going to live there for the next thirty years. You've only been there two years. I'm afraid you've got more navy blood in you than you realize.

The last bit of information may come as something of a shock. I thought about letting you hear it from someone else but decided that would be cruel. I heard through the grapevine Brand Davis is engaged to Catherine Fredrickson. Apparently they've been friends for a long time. I'm sorry if this news hurts you, baby, but I thought you'd want to know.

Have a good time opening up that box of goodies your mother and I mailed.

Love,

Dad

Erin didn't feel anything. Nothing whatsoever. So Brand was marrying Catherine. It was what Erin herself had suggested months earlier. He certainly hadn't allowed any grass to grow under his feet, she mused somewhat bitterly.

A numbing pain took hold and, deciding to ignore it, Erin set aside the mail and fixed herself a dinner consisting of soup and a turkey sandwich. When she finished, she stared at the bowl and plate and decided she couldn't force herself to eat it. Watching television had lost its appeal, too.

Being alone felt intolerable, and she decided to go for a drive. Mingling with other people seemed important all of a sudden.

She wandered through a small shopping complex close to her house, bought a couple of cards at the Hallmark store and strolled back to the parking lot.

"Brand is marrying Catherine," she said aloud in the confines of her car as she drove home. "More than anything, I want him to be happy." She had to say it aloud to remind herself that it was true.

Erin drove past the street where she should have turned off, but for some unknown reason she continued driving, her destination unclear.

An hour passed, and when she found herself close to Aimee's she decided her subconscious was telling her she needed to talk over Brand's engagement with her best friend.

Although Aimee's car was parked in front of her house, she didn't answer the doorbell for several minutes. When she did appear, she was dressed in her housecoat and slippers.

"Erin?" she cried after opening the door. "What are you doing here? Good grief, you look like you've seen a ghost. Come on in." She skillfully steered her through the living room and into the kitchen.

It seemed to Erin that Aimee didn't want her in the living room, which was preposterous, but in case she was arriving at a bad time she asked, "Should I come back later?"

"Of course not," Aimee returned quickly.

A little too quickly, Erin thought. "You look like you were taking a bath."

"No . . . no."

Erin's gaze narrowed suspiciously. "Then why are you wearing a robe?" It wasn't anywhere near time for bed.

Aimee glanced down at the purple velvet as if she'd never seen it before. "Ah . . ."

"Aimee," Erin whispered heatedly. A sinking feeling attacked the pit of her stomach, and she looked around. "Have you got a man in your bedroom?"

The dedicated social worker squeezed her eyes closed and nodded several times.

"Why didn't you say something?" Erin felt like a complete idiot. She wanted to crawl under the carpet and hide.

"I couldn't say anything," Aimee protested at length. "You wouldn't drop by unexpectedly like this unless it was something important. One look at you, and I knew you were upset."

"I'm more upset now than I was before I arrived. It would have been better if you hadn't answered the door."

"May I remind you that you're my best friend," Aimee countered heatedly, although they both continued to whisper in an effort not to be overheard by the mystery man in Aimee's bedroom.

Erin couldn't be more surprised by her friend's actions had she announced she was considering entering a convent. To the best of Erin's knowledge, Aimee had never fooled around. She'd been asked out on a date once or twice but had always declined, claiming she wasn't ready for the singles scene just yet.

It wouldn't be the first time Aimee had surprised her, but until now the surprises had all been pleasant ones. Her friend's divorce was only days from being finalized. Perhaps the pain of what was happening between her and Steve had led her friend into an act completely out of character.

For some time now, Erin had sensed that something was developing in Aimee's life, but she wouldn't have suspected for the world that it was another man. Aimee had given up smoking and was calmer than she had been a few months earlier. Erin had attributed the changes to part of the healing process.

"It's not what you're thinking," Aimee muttered, chastising Erin with a single look. She glanced over her shoulder. "Steve, kindly come out here and save my reputation."

"Steve?" Erin repeated, stunned. "You and Steve? You're divorcing him, remember?"

"Yes, me and Steve," Aimee confirmed. "Steve," she called a second time.

"Honey, if I come out now, I may save your reputation, but it sure as hell will ruin mine."

Aimee actually blushed. Erin couldn't believe it. Her best friend's cheeks went a bright shade of pink.

"Steve?" Erin repeated Aimee's husband's name, still unable to believe what she was hearing.

Aimee nodded, then walked over to the kitchen counter and assembled a pot of coffee.

"You and Steve are . . ." Erin motioned with her hand, as if that would complete the sentence for her. A tardy smile quivered at the corners of her mouth. "When did all this get started?"

"Will you kindly quit looking at me like you're going to burst out laughing?"

"I can't help it. The last time you mentioned Steve's name it was to claim he was involved with another woman. What about the white car parked outside his apartment? You were convinced he wore that ugly green tie to the settlement hearing to irritate you, and —"

"That was before," Aimee reminded her. "That car belonged to his brother, and hell, I should have known better. I was eager to leap to all the wrong conclusions."

"As I recall, you two were finished, and you couldn't wait to sign the final papers."

"We still might."

"What?" Aimee was certainly full of shocking surprises this evening.

"We were talking about it earlier. It might

be wise to start on fresh ground — bury the past, so to speak. We haven't decided yet, but we're leaning toward staying married for . . . for a couple of reasons."

"But what happened to change everything?"

A slow, almost silly smile lit up Aimee's eyes. "About a month ago —"

"A month?" Erin echoed in strained disbelief. It was hard to imagine that she hadn't suspected something earlier. The two were best friends, and Erin felt she really knew Aimee. "You two have been chummy for a month?"

"Longer, actually," Aimee admitted, keeping her voice low. "Steve called about six weeks ago, needing to come over to the house and pick up some things. The atmosphere was cool between us then, to say the least. We arranged a time suitable to us both. I wasn't keen on being here alone with him, but someone had to be here. I didn't trust him not to take more than what he'd come for, and so I gritted my teeth and met him myself."

"You should have asked me." As matters had turned out, Erin was grateful her friend hadn't.

"I know," Aimee agreed, "but it was shortly after Brand left, and you were still so raw. I didn't want to burden you with my problems."

"We've been burdening each other for a good long time. But go on. I'm dying to find out what happened."

Aimee smiled. It was the same silly smile as before. "It got worse before it got better. Actually, it got a whole lot worse. Steve arrived, and we got in this huge fight about a light fixture, of all things. I told him he could have the stupid thing. He claimed he didn't want it, but I refused to let that pass. He was still arguing with me when I dragged out the chair and started to remove it from the wall."

"Aimee!"

"I know, I know. My expertise doesn't involve anything electrical, which Steve took delight in reminding me. At the moment, I think, he was hoping I'd electrocute myself. Fortunately, I fell before that happened."

"You fell?"

"Conveniently into Steve's arms, and we both went crashing to the floor. I was furious and outraged and blamed him. I started listing his legion of faults, and he kissed me just to shut me up so he could see if I'd been hurt."

The picture that formed in Erin's mind was a wildly romantic one. Aimee hopping mad, and Steve more interested in making sure she hadn't been hurt in the fall than in listening to her tirade.

"One thing led to another, and before we

knew it we were in bed together."

"Oh, Aimee that's so romantic."

"Romantic, nothing. I was furious, claiming he'd seduced me. Steve adamantly denied it and said I was the one who'd seduced him. Before the night was over, we'd seduced each other a second time. Both of us were more than a little chagrined over what happened. Steve left the following morning without taking any of the things he claimed he needed so badly. I called him the next day, and he returned for the items . . . only he ended up spending the night again."

"But what about everything that led up to the divorce? You were miserable together. Remember?"

"Nothing's really changed," Aimee explained. "Only our attitude has. We're committed to working out our problems. Steve's willing to see a counselor. In fact, he's the one who suggested it."

"So you've talked everything out?"

"We talked, among other things," Steve inserted as he walked into the kitchen. Standing behind Aimee, he slipped his arms around her waist and cuddled her close. "Should we tell her?" he asked his wife.

"Nothing's for sure yet," Aimee said, twisting her head around to look up at him.

"I'm sure of it."

Erin hadn't a clue what the two were discussing. "Tell me what?"

"Aimee's pregnant. At least we think she is."

"Steve, I haven't been to the doctor yet. You can't go around announcing it until I've been in to see Dr. Larson."

"All those pregnancy test kits you bought claim you are. That's good enough for me." He broke away from his wife and strutted around the kitchen in a walk that would have done a rooster proud.

Delight brightened Aimee's eyes as she held out her hands to Erin. "After ten years. I can't believe it. We tried so hard and for so long." Her face broke into an eager smile. "Oh, Erin, I'm going to have a baby."

The two gripped hands, and Erin felt tears of shared happiness fill her eyes.

"Hey, you two, kindly give credit where credit is due." A light shone in Steven's eyes, one that had been decidedly missing the other times Erin had seen him.

"I couldn't be happier for the two of you," Erin said, sincerely meaning every word, but at the same time the pain she felt knowing Brand was marrying Catherine felt like a heavy chain tightening around her heart. First Terry, and now Aimee.

"You didn't come over here because you suspected anything was developing between Steve and me," Aimee reminded her, scooting out a chair at the table. By now the coffee had brewed, and Aimee automatically brought down mugs.

Steve kissed his wife's cheek. "I'll leave you two to talk," he said, and smiled warmly at Erin before returning to the living room.

"Brand's engaged," Erin announced, her voice trembling slightly. "My dad wrote and told me. He claimed it was better I hear the news from him than someone else."

"Oh, Erin, I'm so sorry."

"What's to be sorry about?" she asked with a shaky laugh. "If marrying Catherine is what it takes to make Brand happy, then why should I feel bad?"

"You love him."

"I know."

Aimee was quiet for a moment. "Have you given any more thought to what I said all those weeks ago about having our jobs taint our views on marriage?"

Erin hadn't. She'd been sifting through so much emotion and pain that she'd filed her friend's thoughts away in the farthest corner of her mind. "Not really."

"Then do. Not all marriages end in misery and heartache."

"It sometimes seems that way."

"I know," Aimee was quick to agree. "Think about it, Erin. You haven't been at this job long enough to gain perspective yet. That comes with time. I fell into that same trap myself.

"There are plenty of good marriages out

there that work because the two people involved are prepared to do whatever they have to to see that it does."

Erin drew in a deep breath. "It's too late now for Brand and me."

"That's what I thought," Aimee reminded her.

"I want Brand to marry Catherine," Erin murmured, telling the biggest lie of her life. "They're perfect together . . . I said so from the first."

A Christmas card to Brand wouldn't hurt, Erin decided later. One with a brief note of congratulations. It took her nearly three days to compose the few lines.

Dear Brand,
Merry Christmas. I always claimed you and Catherine were perfect together. Now Dad tells me he heard through the grapevine that the two of you have set the big date. Congratulations.

I honestly mean that. I wish you only the best. You deserve it.

                                        Erin

P.S. Neal and I are getting along famously.

Neal, Brand mused, reading over the short message a second time. He didn't know what

299

tricks Erin was up to now, but he wasn't in the mood for it. He'd put her out of his life, and he was managing nicely.

"Who the hell are you kidding?" he asked out loud.

"You say something?" Romano asked.

"Nothing that concerns you," Brand barked. "Who the hell leaked out information about me and Catherine?"

"What kind of information?"

"That we're marrying."

"Hell, I don't know who'd say anything. Is it true?"

Brand answered that with a single intense look.

"Hey, don't get mad at me. I was just asking." Alex scooted away from his desk. "What's with you today, anyway?"

Brand debated on whether he'd let his friend know or not, then decided he owed everyone around him an explanation. He hadn't been the best company the past few weeks. "I got a Christmas card from Erin."

Romano responded with a low whistle. "No wonder you've been acting like a wounded bear all day. What'd she have to say?"

"Congratulations to me and Cath," he answered with a low snicker.

"You going to write and let her know the truth?"

"No," Brand answered without hesitating. If Erin wanted to believe he was marrying

Catherine, he'd let her.

"I take it you don't plan on looking her up next week, either?"

"Hell, no." Brand had cursed the assignment that was taking him into Seattle. The timing couldn't have been worse. Two months, and he was only now getting to the point that he could go a small portion of the day without dwelling on the situation between him and Erin. He wasn't about to set himself up for more pain. He'd had all he could take.

Brand altered that decision, however, shortly after he checked into the Seattle hotel. He had a rental car, and with time to kill he decided it wouldn't hurt to swing past Erin's house. If luck was with him, he might catch a glimpse of her.

Luck, however, hadn't exactly been tossing charms his way lately, he was quick to note.

"You're acting like a lovesick fool," he told himself as he exited from the freeway and climbed the twisting roadway that led to West Seattle. "Why the hell shouldn't you?" He asked himself next. "You've been a lovesick fool from the moment you met Erin MacNamera."

By the time he was on the side street that led to her house, Brand was having third and fourth thoughts. They vanished the minute he saw the For Sale sign.

He waited until the blazing anger that

raged through him had dissipated enough for him to think clearly. When it had, he stepped out of the car and marched to her front door and rapped hard against the wooden structure.

She took her sweet time answering. Her complexion went pale when she saw him, and his name was only a voiceless movement of her lips.

"What's that For Sale sign doing on the front lawn?" he demanded.

Erin looked up at him as if she were sorely tempted to reach out and touch him to be sure he wasn't a figment of her imagination.

"The For Sale sign," he repeated harshly, pointing to it in case she wasn't aware it was there.

"I'm selling the house," she whispered, then blinked twice. "What are you doing here?"

"I'm on assignment. I want to know why the hell you're moving."

"It's . . . well, it's not easy to explain."

She stepped aside for him to come into the house. Brand had no intention of doing so. He was walking a fine line as it was. His anger had carried him all the way to her front door, but being this close to Erin, loving her as much as he did and loathing her for the hell she'd put him through, wasn't exactly conducive to them being alone together. He'd forgotten how beautiful she was, with her rich auburn hair and her expressive dark eyes. They registered a multitude of emotions.

"I can't . . . explain it out here," she said when he doggedly remained where he was. "Come inside. There's coffee."

"If you don't mind, I'd prefer not to. Just kindly tell me why you're moving?"

"You don't want to come inside?" Erin sounded hurt and incredulous.

"No." Once again he pointed to the sign.

"I have to sell," she explained haltingly. "Well, I don't exactly have to . . . Actually, if you want the truth, I'm sick of the grand piano. It takes up the entire living room, I don't have the time for lessons, and I lack talent."

"That isn't any reason to sell. A few months ago a bulldozer was the only thing that would get you out of this house."

"It isn't the house that was so important to me."

"Then what the hell was it?"

"Roots," she shouted back, just as angry and impatient with him as he was with her.

Brand wasn't buying that for one minute. "Now we both know, don't we, Erin? All this business about needing security was bull. You don't have any more roots in Seattle than you did anyplace else. You can pretend all you want after today, sweetheart, but for right now, you're going to admit the truth."

She frowned as if she hadn't a clue what he was saying.

"You're bored and restless," he elaborated.

She denied that with a hard shake of her head. "That's not true."

"Sorry, sweetheart, I should have recognized the symptoms, but I was so damn much in love with you, a battleship would have escaped me."

A lone tear ran down the side of her face, but Brand was in no mood to react to her anguish. Perhaps deep down he was pleased to see her crying, although he didn't like to think that was true. She'd put him through hell, and if she was suffering a little, then so much the better.

"You thrive on change, you always have, only you refused to admit it. You're looking for a challenge, because it's the only thing you've ever known. You grew up learning how to adjust to situations, and now all of a sudden there's nothing new. Everything is the same, one day after the next, and you're looking for a way out, only you're sugar-coating it with the idea that you don't have enough room in your living room. Did it ever occur to you that you might sell the piano?"

"No," she whispered in a tight, strained voice.

"I didn't think it would." She thought

more like a navy wife than Brand had ever realized.

Neither of them spoke for several tense moments. Brand knew he should turn and walk away from her. He'd said everything he wanted to and more. Erin stood before him as pale as a canvas sail bleached by the sun, holding herself proud, her head high and regal.

He started to move, but every step felt as if he were dragging an anchor with him. Part of him yearned to shout back at her, tell her she'd never find a man who loved her as much as he did, but she'd rejected his love once, and he was too damn proud to hand her the power to injure him again.

He was halfway to his car when she called out to him. "Brand . . ."

He twisted around and discovered that she'd walked down the steps toward him. "What?" he demanded brusquely.

She shook her head. Then, using the back of her hands, she wiped the moisture from her face. "I'm so —"

"Don't apologize," he said, in as cutting a voice as he could manage. He could take anything but that. She didn't want him, didn't love him enough. By God, he wasn't about to let her water down her regrets by telling him how sorry she was.

"I wasn't," she whispered brokenly. "Just be happy."

Something broke within Brand, something deep and fundamental that had been wounded that afternoon in the Seattle hotel. "Be happy," he shouted, marching up to her. He gripped her hard by the shoulders. The power of the emotion had a stranglehold on all his good intentions to turn and aloofly walk away from her. He had damn little pride left when it came to Erin, but for once he was determined to close himself off from her. After all the times she'd hurt him, it felt good to be the one in control. He struggled to remain indifferent and detached.

He ruined everything by announcing the truth. "Do you honestly believe I can be happy without you in my life?" he demanded. "Fat chance, sweetheart."

She blinked up at him, her eyes stricken and wide. "But you're marrying Catherine."

He snickered loudly. "Your father should know by now not to trust everything he hears."

"You mean you're not?"

"Not anytime soon," he bit out caustically.

Indescribable joy crowded Erin's face before she gave a hoarse shriek. She tossed her arms around his neck and shocked him by spreading madcap kisses all over his face. Her hands were splayed over his ears as her sweet mouth bestowed a fleeting succession of kisses wherever her lips happened to land. Tears mingled with those first kisses and mumbled, unintelligible words.

"Erin, stop," he demanded. At the first touch of her mouth, the hard protective shell he'd erected around his heart cracked. He'd worked like a madman to fortify it from the moment he'd knocked on her front door. He didn't know how much longer he could hold out with her touching him like this.

Her lips found his, and he opened to her, hungry and eager and too battle-weary to fight her any longer. He took control of the kiss, plowing his hands into her hair and slanting his mouth over hers. She sighed and locked her arms around his neck and kissed him back with a need that made Brand bitterly regret the fact they were outside her house.

"You're going to marry me," he told her forcefully.

"Yes . . . yes," she answered, as if there had never been any question about it. "Only let's make the wedding soon."

Brand frowned. He couldn't believe what he was hearing. "I'm probably going to get transferred."

"I know."

"In the next twenty years I may be stationed from here to kingdom come. We'll move any number of times."

"No doubt we will, but I'm used to that."

The rigid control he'd maintained early on had melted and puddled at his feet, but

307

Brand wasn't completely convinced this was for real. He wasn't leaving anything to speculation. "There are going to be children."

"I certainly hope so."

"You wanted roots, remember?"

"I've got them, only they're wound around you."

Brand felt dizzy with relief and a profound sense of completeness. "Why?"

She laughed softly, and he heard the pain mingled with the joy. "You're right . . . you were right all along, only I was too blind to realize it. For months I've been restless and bored, just like you said. I wanted to blame that feeling on you, but it started long before we met. Nearly every weekend I was taking long drives. Last month I put the house on the market, thinking once it sold I'd put in my notice at the office and move to Oregon.

"I was wrong about so many things. Aimee was right — I hadn't been with the Community Action Program long enough to realize some marriages do work. People can stay in love forever. I'd forgotten that and so many other things. Did you know I attended four different universities? Can you believe that? All along I kept claiming I wanted roots, but I was too blind to see how bored I get in one place. When I did realize that, it was too late — I'd heard about you and Catherine. Oh, Brand, I'm so ready to be your wife. So ready to settle down."

"The only place you're going to settle is with me."

"Aye, aye, Lieutenant," she whispered. Her mouth claimed his for a lengthy series of delicate, nibbling kisses.

Epilogue

"Here we are again," a smiling Ginger Romano commented to Erin as they stood on the crowded pier. The two were part of a large gathering of family members waiting for the crew of the *Blue Ridge* to disembark after a lengthy cruise. The ship was returning from monitoring sea trials and had been gone nearly five months.

Erin was eager for Brand's return for more than the usual reasons. She'd missed her husband the way she always missed him when he was away for any length of time. They'd been blissfully happy in the two years since their marriage. Becoming Brand's wife had taught Erin several valuable lessons about herself. She loved navy life. Thrived on it, just the way he'd claimed she would. She was home, where she'd always meant to be. The navy was in her blood, the same way it was in her father's and in Brand's. She might not have a whole lot to do with national defense, but she, and the other wives like her, were as important to the navy as the entire Pacific fleet.

"There's Daddy," Ginger shrieked, pointing to Alex as he walked down the gangplank. Bobby and the two little ones went racing toward their father.

Brand was directly behind Alex. He paused and searched the crowd for Erin. Her heart sped as she started toward him at a dignified gait. Soon, however, she broke into a run as Brand started rushing toward her. He caught her by the waist and lifted her high above his head; their mouths found and clung to each other in a love feast of longing and need.

"Welcome home, Lieutenant," she said when she could, wiping the moisture from her face. Generally she wasn't emotional at these reunions, and she didn't want to give away her secret too quickly.

Slowly Brand lowered her to the ground, but he didn't release her. "You missed me?"

"Like crazy."

"You're pale." His hand tenderly caressed her cheek. "You haven't been overdoing this volunteer work, have you?"

"I love working with the Chaplain's Office."

"That didn't answer my question."

"Quit arguing and kindly kiss me."

Brand was all too eager to comply, pulling her flush against him, his mouth greedy over hers. When he raised his head, his eyes were narrowed and questioning.

"Erin?"

"Yes." She smiled saucily up at him.

"You've gained weight?"

"Is that a question or a statement?"

He stepped back from her, and Erin

311

watched as his gaze shifted from her swollen breasts to the slight swell of her smoothly rounded stomach. He splayed his fingers over the mound and stared at her as if he'd never seen a pregnant woman in his entire life.

"Yes, my darling, we're pregnant."

"A baby," he whispered haltingly. "But . . . you never said a word."

"I didn't find out until after you'd left, and then I thought a pregnant wife would make a delightful surprise for your homecoming."

"A baby," he whispered a second time, and seemed to be struggling for words. He gently cupped her face in his hands and brushed the pads of his thumbs across the slick tears that streamed down her cheeks. "I love you, Erin MacNamera Davis, more and more each day. Thank God you came to your senses and married me."

Erin thanked God, too. Her husband's large hand flattened across her abdomen as he brought her protectively into the circle of his arms. "A baby," he whispered, as if he still couldn't believe it was true.

"Our own navy brat," Erin added, just before their mouths merged.